A Game of Fox & Squirrels

JENN REESE

with illustrations by Jessica Roux

Henry Holt and Company

New York

Henry Holt and Company, *Publishers since 1866*
Henry Holt® is a registered trademark of Macmillan Publishing Group, LLC
120 Broadway, New York, NY 10271 • mackids.com

Library of Congress Control Number: 2019940952
ISBN 978-1-250-24301-0 (hardcover) / ISBN 978-1-250-24302-7 (ebook)

Our books may be purchased in bulk for promotional, educational, or business use.
Please contact your local bookseller or the Macmillan Corporate and Premium Sales
Department at (800) 221-7945 ext. 5442 or by email at
MacmillanSpecialMarkets@macmillan.com.

First edition, 2020 / Designed by Mallory Grigg
Printed in the United States of America by LSC Communications,
Harrisonburg, Virginia

10 9 8 7 6 5 4 3 2 1

For everyone lost in the woods:
I promise you, there is a way out.

And for my found family, who was mine.

Chapter One

SAMANTHA LITTLEFIELD SAT alone in the back seat of the car for the whole ride from the airport. Her suitcase and backpack were in the trunk, which meant she didn't have her books, her comics, her notebook and pens. What was even left? Sam hugged the thin fabric of her shirt and stared out the window. This wasn't how she should be spending the week of her eleventh birthday. A bear sighting might cheer her up. Or a moose. But only trees blurred by, tall sentinels on both sides of the road as far as she could see. How would she ever sneak past them when it was time to leave?

In the front of the car, Aunt Vicky asked Sam's older sister, Caitlin, another question. Aunt Vicky was a large woman, but her voice was small. A moth voice, fluttering and easy to miss unless you leaned in, listened harder. Sam leaned away instead.

She pressed her forehead to the window glass. It was cooler here than back home in Los Angeles, where the temperature had been in the 90s for months. Oregon was supposed to have "more moderate summers." That's what their caseworker—Mrs. Washington—had said, like it was some big selling point. Mrs. Washington had wanted Sam to be excited about getting on the plane, had wanted Sam to stop thinking about leaving her parents. Caitlin had played along. Caitlin *always* played along. *That sounds wonderful, Mrs. Washington! I'm sure we'll love it.*

But Sam *liked* the heat. She'd never known anything else. She already missed it.

The tree-guards along the side of the road laughed, their branchy shoulders rustling. Oh, they were arrogant, those trees. Thinking they were so high and mighty just because they were, well, literally high and mighty.

Aunt Vicky turned off the main road. The car grumbled and juddered along a narrow dirt path. A blue-green house emerged around the next bend, and with it a fenced yard containing a miniature house painted to match the big one.

"Chickens!" Caitlin exclaimed from the front seat.

Sam leaned forward, eagerly scanning the yard. Sure enough, a cluster of mottled white-and-black birds bobbed and strutted in the grass. Chickens! And the tiny house was a chicken coop!

"We have six chickens," Aunt Vicky said. "They give us our eggs. You can help gather them. If you want."

Sam did not know what was involved with gathering eggs, but even so, she *did* want. The only time she'd ever touched a chicken was at a petting zoo. Its feathers had been so soft, its eyes so surprisingly fierce in its tiny head. Sam could have

2

petted that chicken forever, but Caitlin had been eager to see the horse. Sam glanced at her sister now, hoping Caitlin's chicken excitement was mostly real.

"Gathering eggs sounds cool!" Caitlin said, and Sam almost cheered. Aunt Vicky's smile brightened immediately.

Sam wished she shared Caitlin's skill at talking to adults. It seemed like something you were born with, like blond hair or the ability to touch your nose with your tongue. Caitlin had gotten all the dealing-with-adults skills and Sam had gotten ... what? A few freckles, maybe. Some molars prone to cavities. It hardly seemed fair.

The car rolled to a stop. Caitlin fumbled with her car door, but Sam didn't move. She had no interest in getting out, in setting foot in *Oregon*. She'd rather just watch the chickens. One bird was larger than the rest and seemed to know it. Maybe she was a great chicken warrior, the One Chosen Chicken, destined to lead all the other chickens into an epic battle of good versus—

"That big one is Lady Louise. She's a bully, but she lays the best eggs," Aunt Vicky said, unbuckling her seat belt and twisting to see Sam. Aunt Vicky only looked a little like Sam's dad, despite them being siblings. Her skin was the same shade of sandy white, but she didn't wear glasses and her hair was brown instead of blond. Brown like Sam's. There was something different about her eyes, too, but Sam dropped her gaze before she could figure out what it was.

"Do you . . . like chickens?" Aunt Vicky asked her.

Yes yes yes.

Sam shrugged. It was the fastest way to get someone to stop looking at her.

Caitlin hopped out of the car. "It's so beautiful here! The air smells so clean." She raised her good arm and twirled around. And just like that, all eyes were on Caitlin again. Sometimes not even Sam could tell when her sister was doing it on purpose, drawing all the attention. She was grateful for it regardless.

Sam quietly extracted herself from the back seat and stood in the gravel driveway. She took a deep breath, trying to smell what Caitlin smelled, trying to feel what Caitlin felt. It didn't usually work, but she had to admit there *was* something different about the air here. A taste. A *flavor*. She wasn't sure if she liked it.

An envelope fell out of her pocket. Sam swooped it up quickly, once again admiring the horse and rainbow her friend BriAnn had drawn on the front with bright colored pencils. She was such a great artist. Inside, BriAnn had detailed every single minute of her family's trip to Oklahoma for her cousin's wedding, including a sketch of the bride's flowery dress and her cousin's tuxedo, complete with arrows and commentary. Sam knew that as soon as BriAnn got back to Los Angeles, she would want to know why Sam wasn't around.

Maybe Sam would say she went to Hawaii with her family.

A last-minute trip before school started in two weeks. It certainly sounded more believable than the truth.

The front door of the house flapped open, and a lumberjack appeared. Well, a tall, wiry woman dressed like a lumberjack, wearing jeans and a red flannel shirt even though it was summer. Her hair was short and spiky and black with a tiny bit of gray at her temples. She was smiling as she headed straight for the trunk and the bags Aunt Vicky was unloading.

"Let me get those," the woman said. "How was the drive?"

"Fine," Aunt Vicky said, and handed Sam's backpack to the woman. The woman casually slung it over her shoulder as if it didn't contain Sam's most treasured possessions and then touched Aunt Vicky's arm. A look passed between them so fast they probably thought no one saw. But Sam noticed. She bet Caitlin did, too. Were they upset? Had Sam already done something wrong? She shrank against the side of the car, trying to stay out of the way.

"Can I help carry anything?" Caitlin asked. "Oh, wait. I forgot." She hefted her broken arm as if she had, until this moment, forgotten that it was broken. That was always how Caitlin handled these situations, by making herself bigger even as Sam disappeared.

"No, sweetie, I've got it all," the woman said.

Who was this person who was taking all their things and who hadn't even been introduced? Aunt Vicky stood by the open trunk, not moving, her eyebrows knit together.

The woman noticed that Aunt Vicky was in a daze. "I'm Hannah Zhang," she said to Caitlin and Sam. "You can call me Hannah. I'm your aunt's wife. Come on in. I made lemonade and there's at least one box of cookies. They might be stale, but they're still cookies, am I right?"

Mrs. Washington had told them Aunt Vicky was married, and somehow Sam had forgotten. Had forgotten that she'd be staying with *two* new people, not just one. So many things had happened in the past few days that even big things had fallen through the cracks.

"Wow, lemonade and cookies!" Caitlin said. "I'm sure we're going to love it here."

This seemed to shake Aunt Vicky from her stupor. She closed the trunk and walked to the house, her feet barely making any noise on the gravel. "Come on, girls, I'll show you to your rooms, and you can settle in. If you want."

Hannah and Aunt Vicky and Caitlin disappeared inside, one by one. Sam stayed by the car, wanting to avoid the chaos that was sure to unfold in the house: the questions, the offers of food, the general awkwardness of standing in a strange place surrounded by strange people. Caitlin would settle things, figure out the rules, and then it would be safer. Quieter. More manageable.

Instead, Sam watched the chickens pecking at the grass. She listened to the trees laughing. She breathed in the strange, different air.

Oregon.

Los Angeles was in California, and Oregon was only one state north. They shared a border, even. But right now it felt as if she'd fallen down a rabbit hole into another world. She didn't want to be here. She didn't want any of this. She didn't even know she had an Aunt Vicky until a week ago. And now there was Hannah Zhang, too, and trees, and chickens, and all her books and pens and pencils and notebooks were inside already, with as many of her clothes as her mother and her caseworker had been able to fit into one suitcase.

If Sam knew how to drive, she could drive back down to Los Angeles. She could drive to her parents. They would be so impressed and touched that she'd traveled all that way herself. Not even Caitlin could do something like that. To celebrate, they'd walk to Ventura Boulevard and get banana pancakes with walnuts and whipped cream at their favorite breakfast place, and afterward, her dad would drink another cup of coffee and work on the crossword while Sam browsed the used books in the shop next door. And maybe then—

Aunt Vicky stepped onto the porch, shattering Sam's daydream. She wore long shorts that fell over her knees and an oversized gray T-shirt with nothing on it, no pictures or funny phrases or logos. Not a single clue to tell Sam who this mysterious aunt was, what she liked, or what sorts of things would make her upset.

"Are you okay?" Aunt Vicky asked.

The question startled Sam. Startled her so much that before she could figure out why, she shuffled across the gravel to the house and followed Aunt Vicky inside.

From the driveway, the house had looked squat and run-down, its slanted roof covered in moss as if the forest were trying to slowly digest it and no one particularly minded. Inside, it was mostly the same. The kitchen was tiny and cramped, with stacks of mugs and plates just sitting on the countertop because there was, apparently, no room for them in the moss-green cabinets. Sam passed a main room with a television and a sofa and a table, and then a door to a bathroom, and then, finally, her aunt pushed open the door at the end of the hallway and said, "This is your room, Samantha."

Sam's chest tightened. The room was smaller than her bedroom back home and already crammed with stuff. A work table had been shoved against the wall and was stacked with plastic boxes, almost all the way up to the ceiling. Aunt Vicky opened the closet to reveal more rows and columns of the same plastic bins. "We'll clear this out so you have room for your clothes," she said. "I still have to find somewhere to put everything."

Sam tried to see what was in the plastic containers. Art supplies? Thousands of pieces of tiny doll clothes? The pickled organs of everyone else who'd ever stayed in this room?

"There are two empty drawers in the dresser," Aunt Vicky said, as if this was some kind of victory. "We'll figure it out.

We'll figure it all out." She mumbled the last bit under her breath like a spell.

The bed was covered in a multihued quilt made from every shade of blue, and two flat pillows sat stacked at the far end in sad white pillowcases. A wrapped package at the foot of the bed caught Sam's attention.

"Is this for me?" She picked it up, pulled the long pink ribbon through her fingers.

"Happy birthday," Aunt Vicky said. "It was yesterday, wasn't it? I thought you might like a present. We can bake a cake later, too. With frosting. I'm not sure if we have enough sugar, but we definitely have the eggs." She chuckled, but Sam didn't know why.

Oh, the chickens. Eggs and chickens. Eggs and cakes. Chickens and cakes. Was this the sort of thing people in Oregon found funny? If so, it was going to be a very long visit.

A visit. Just a visit.

"Open it," her aunt said, then quickly amended, "if you want to." She sat on the edge of the bed, clearly eager to watch the unwrapping.

Sam ripped off the paper and gasped. It wasn't a book, as she'd been expecting. *A Game of Fox & Squirrels* was written in faded type across a battered box. The ampersand was swirly and inviting, and Sam couldn't help but run her fingertip along its wild, swooping curves.

Something moved outside the window. A flash of red, fast

as a heartbeat. But when Sam looked, she saw only the same old green grass and trees and blue sky.

"It's a card game," Aunt Vicky said. "Works better with a few people. We can play later, if you want."

Sam gave Aunt Vicky a quick smile. "Thanks. It looks really interesting." And she meant it. She traced the design on the box again, and a tingle scurried up her spine. There was something special about this game. She could tell. Maybe something a little bit *magic*.

From the Rules for Fox & Squirrels

INTRODUCTION

Winter is fast approaching, and you, brave squirrel, must prepare!

Your survival depends on finding and storing nuts for the cold months to come. You will do this by collecting "sets" and "runs" of cards. So simple!

But there's a catch. Isn't there always?

In this game, that catch is the FOX.

Chapter Two

"LEMONADE!" HANNAH SANG. Literally sang, with notes and everything.

"And at least four—no, five—cookies," Aunt Vicky added.

"Hurry up, or I'll eat them all myself," Hannah said.

Sam walked softly to the main part of the house, which seemed to be the kitchen and dining room and living room all in one. Aunt Vicky and Hannah bustled back and forth, pouring lemonade into glasses, finding plates and napkins, pulling boxes from the cupboards. They reminded Sam of the chickens in the yard, always moving.

Caitlin sat at a long wooden table that seemed to be part kitchen table, part office, judging from all the computer equipment at one end. Her good hand was wrapped around a sweating glass of lemonade. Sam perched on a chair next to her, ready to bolt back to her room if necessary. Caitlin gave her a quick nod of encouragement, and Sam settled a little more into her seat.

"Cookies?" Aunt Vicky asked, shaking a mostly empty box of Thin Mints at Sam. "I finished off the peanut butter ones last week, before I knew you were coming. Sorry about that."

Sam stared at the box of cookies. Maybe this was some sort of fairy test, and if she ate the food here, she'd have to stay forever.

She shook her head.

Aunt Vicky rattled the cardboard again. "Okay. There's still lemonade. And cake later, if you want. But after dinner! We don't only eat sweets around here, even if it seems like it."

"I could live off pie," Hannah said casually. "There are so many different kinds. I don't know why you'd need to eat anything else."

"I'm a little tired," Caitlin said with a yawn. "Would it be okay if I took a nap in my room?"

"Certainly," Hannah said at the same time Aunt Vicky blurted, "Of course!" They both exploded into action, pulling shades and depositing suitcases and delivering secondary glasses of lemonade to both their rooms. Sam pressed her back to the wall and tried to stay out of their way.

"Can I help with the dishes?" Caitlin asked.

Sam hid a smile. There were no dishes. Such was Caitlin's brilliance.

Hannah beamed. "Absolutely not! You go rest after that long flight."

The drive had been longer than the flight, but Sam didn't say so. Caitlin thanked them both for the lemonade and went to her room without even looking back. Sam realized, almost too late, that if she didn't escape now, Aunt Vicky and Hannah would turn their attentions on *her*.

She followed her sister before anyone could stop her. But before returning to her own assigned room, she pushed open the door to Caitlin's.

A treadmill, folded up and shoved against the wall, stood guard next to the nightstand. The bed itself was new, the white headboard the only thing in the house that wasn't covered in a layer of dust. Caitlin was older, almost fourteen and about to start high school. It made sense for her to get the new bed and the room that wasn't filled with bins and boxes and someone else's life.

Caitlin flopped onto the bed, fumbled with her headphones, and closed her eyes. Muffled music tumbled out of them, an upbeat rhythm with a woman's raspy voice overlaid. Without even opening her eyes, Caitlin said, "Get out."

"I just wanted to see your room," Sam said from the doorway.

"You've seen it. Now get out." Caitlin's toe bopped in time with the music.

Sam tried again. "Is your arm doing better today?"

Caitlin sighed dramatically but then, much to Sam's surprise, actually answered. "It's a pain, but it's not, you know, actually *painful* anymore. Just forget about it."

As if Sam could do that, could just forget about what had happened. But she knew better than to press Caitlin about it now. And besides, there was a more important question weighing on her mind. "When . . . when do you think we can go back?"

Caitlin's eyes popped open. "Try to forget about that, too." She shut them again.

Sam stood awkwardly in the doorway for another minute, waiting to see if Caitlin would say anything else, but that was it. When Caitlin wanted to forget something, she did.

Her own room seemed smaller after seeing Caitlin's. The boxes were everywhere, great imposing stacks of them. Although—she tilted her head—the way all the plastic bins were stacked, they almost looked like the stones of a castle wall.

Yes. She could see it now.

The bins in the closet were the most promising. Sam pulled out the ones in the middle and stacked them to the sides. She worked slowly, careful not to make any noise. And she didn't open any of them—moving the bins represented a certain level of trouble, but opening them . . . well, that was just *asking* for it. Aunt Vicky was big and Hannah looked strong and Sam had no desire to make them angry. *You brought this on yourself.* Not on her first day. Not when she didn't even know how long she had to stay here.

Sam arranged the bins like a medieval stonemason, building her new structure with a critical eye. It felt strangely good to be using her body after hours of sitting on the plane and in the car, after days of sitting in plastic chairs while adults talked above and around her, while doctors hovered over Caitlin in her hospital bed, while people whispered and glanced and tried not to point. Until last week, she hadn't realized that sitting could be so exhausting.

But she wasn't sitting now—she was *working*. Soon Sam had carved out the center of the closet bins, leaving two walls that reached out into the room. It took her six tries to throw the bed quilt over the top to make a roof, but then she had it.

A fort.

A *castle* fort.

She lined it with the pillows from the bed. Back home, her pillows had been fluffier, all four of them deep-sea blue with a tiny dolphin-and-shell pattern. They were probably still on her bed, probably still arranged exactly how she had left them, along with the rest of her things. She imagined her room like Sleeping Beauty's Castle—everything in a magical sleep awaiting her return.

She'd always had her own room, ever since she was little, and although her mother had picked the pale-yellow paint of the walls, Sam had been allowed to cover those walls with posters. She'd found them folded up in the creases of her father's *National Geographic* magazines—he had a collection going back to the early 1900s. The old maps were her favorites. Sometimes on Saturdays, she'd go with her dad to one flea market after another. They'd comb through boxes of stinky, dusty magazines looking for the issues they were missing. Sam kept the official list in a notebook. Any time they found one, they got ice cream to celebrate. And if they didn't find one, they got ice cream anyway.

There were no posters on the walls of Aunt Vicky's room, only a row of small, framed flowers near the door. Nothing interesting. Nothing familiar.

Inside the fort, Sam opened her backpack and pulled out all the books. She arranged them by size along one of her castle walls: the illustrated book of fairy tales on the left, because it was the biggest, all the way down to her paperback copy of *The Hobbit*, dog-eared and ripped and stained, because she never went anywhere without it. There were a few books she hadn't even read yet—one about a girl who was actually a dragon and another about a robot boy and his robot dog. She winced when she saw the spine of the last one. A library book. *That belongs in a library in a whole 'nother state.*

That last night, the night that everything went so awful— *the thud of something hitting the wall*—Sam had been reading this book. Trying to get to the end of a chapter before anyone noticed that she was still awake. Her finger wiggled between the pages where the bookmark was nestled, but she didn't open it. She was afraid of what might happen.

Sometimes Sam's mind took her places she didn't want to go. Someone would ask her a simple question at school, and even though she was standing by her locker, her mind would be back in San Diego on a family vacation at the very moment when *a snarl, a snap. The flash of a fist.*

Sam pulled her finger from the pages and slid the book into place on her makeshift bookshelf. She'd try again later. It wasn't due back at the library for another eight days, and maybe she'd be back home by then anyway.

Back home.

Sam eyed *The Hobbit.* J. R. R. Tolkien's famous book had a second, less well-known name, and it made Sam's chest hurt a little to think of it. The subtitle of *The Hobbit* was *There and Back Again.* Because it wasn't enough for Bilbo Baggins to go on an epic quest across all of middle-earth. He had to go back home again afterward.

Heroes always went home.

Sam's eyes began to prickle, and she looked away. That's when the glittery, golden type on A Game of Fox & Squirrels caught her eye.

Sam fluffed her pillows and settled into her castle nest. She tugged at the faded cardboard tongue of the game box, and it slipped free, eager to spill its secrets. Two stacks of playing cards slid into Sam's palm. The backs bore an ornate forest design in purples and blues. Faded gold birds sang from the branches of a massive central tree, and the silhouettes of a gold fox and squirrel sat on either side of its trunk. What kind of forest was purple instead of green? A fairy forest, maybe. Or a forest in another world. The kind of forest where the animals were all made of gold. Oh, how Sam wanted to see it for herself! It hurt her heart to know places like this existed but that she had no way to reach them.

Something flashed under the bed. Sam started. A golden tail?

No, of course not.

It was only the sunlight reflecting off the shiny surface of the table lamp. It couldn't possibly have been anything else … no matter how much she wanted it to be.

Sam flipped over one of the cards in her hand. The six of spades … except the spade was etched into the body of an acorn at the corner and the six acorns scattered in the middle of the card were being gathered up by a nervous-looking squirrel. She leafed eagerly through the deck. Each suit had a different type of squirrel and a different type of nut: acorns with spades, almonds with diamonds, walnuts with hearts, and peanuts with clubs. Sam sighed. Peanuts weren't actually nuts, they were legumes. Whoever had made the game should have done their research!

It was easy to overlook this small mistake, though, in light of how the cards made Sam feel—like she was looking through a window into another world. The "royal" cards—the queen, king, and page—were particularly handsome, their squirrels decked in tiny robes and crowns. Sam lingered over the Queen of Hearts, whose little squirrel paws were holding a magnificent walnut as if it was the greatest prize in all the kingdom. The squirrel seemed so proud, so regal, that Sam couldn't help smiling and sitting a little straighter herself.

Sam admired each card—touching the noses of the animals, counting the nuts (and legumes!)—until, finally, she reached the end.

And found the Fox.

The Fox was *dashing*. He wore a fancy purple coat lined in gold and carried a satchel. A jaunty feathered hat sat angled on his fuzzy red head. He seemed alive enough to breathe, right there on the card! He could have been a Disney character, except his eyes were regular fox eyes, golden brown and sharp, and not huge cartoonish eyes that took up half his face.

Sam heard a knock at the door and then Aunt Vicky call out, "Dinner."

Her heart burst into rabbit mode. That's what a doctor had called it once, *rabbit mode*, when he was explaining it to Sam's mother. Hearts were supposed to pace themselves as if they were running a marathon—slow and steady like the tortoise in that old fable "The Tortoise and the Hare." But sometimes Sam's heart tried to be the hare, jumping this way and that, frantic and foolish, as if it were trying to escape from her chest.

What if Aunt Vicky opened the door and saw the castle fort? Sam should never have touched her aunt's things, should never have moved them, should never have presumed. Sam clutched the cards in her hand, completely frozen, while her heart raced in wild circles.

But Aunt Vicky didn't open the door, and a moment later Sam heard her knock on Caitlin's door and say the same thing before moving back down the hallway. Sam let out a breath. Aunt Vicky wasn't coming in. She wasn't going to see what Sam had done.

None of that mattered to her rabbit heart, though, which kept hopping and bouncing against her ribs. The doctor—he was the comfy-chairs-in-an-office kind, not the sterile-examining-table-and-stethoscope kind—had given her some exercises, and she tried them now.

Breathe. One, two, three. Breathe. Four, five, six. Breathe. Seven, eight, nine. By the time she got to eighteen, her heart was almost a tortoise again.

Sam wiggled the Fox & Squirrels cards back into their box with shaking hands and shelved the game next to her books along her castle wall. She should dismantle her fort, she knew. It would be safer than leaving it here to be found. She'd gotten lucky this time. She wouldn't always be. She never was.

But Sam left her castle standing, closed the bedroom door behind her, and, like a tortoise, slowly made her way to dinner.

FROM THE RULES FOR FOX & SQUIRRELS

THE FOX

Winter isn't the only thing the squirrel must plan for; there is also the Fox. The Fox can appear at any time.

The Fox might be happy. (Happy foxes are a joy!)

The Fox might be charming. (Charming foxes are a delight!)

But sooner or later . . .

The Fox will be hunting.

CHAPTER THREE

CONDIMENTS SAT IN the center of the kitchen table like a tiny cityscape: ketchup and sriracha soaring above the rest, two thin spires of hot sauce, spice jars plump and low and labeled GARLIC and OREGANO and SHALLOTS. What was a shallot? It sounded dangerous.

The four of them were crammed around one end of the long table because computers occupied the other half, big black monitors arranged like an altar, worshipped by keyboards and mice and surrounded by coils of unkempt black cords.

Sam did not ask about them, and neither did Caitlin. They knew better. Sam slid into the seat next to her sister.

Hannah spooned scrambled eggs onto Sam's plate. Sam's mother only made scrambled eggs for breakfast, and she stirred in cream cheese so they were gooey and soft. Or sometimes she sprinkled sesame seeds on top for a little crunch, or added crumbled crackers to the eggs before she cooked them. Hannah's scrambled eggs were just eggs.

But at least Hannah sat at the table once she was done cooking. Aunt Vicky kept popping up to go to the fridge, or to take a glass to the sink, or to "grab another napkin." Like she could hardly stand the thought of sitting for more than five seconds at a time.

"The eggs are delicious," Caitlin said. "Did you use special spices?"

Hannah smiled, clearly happy to be asked. "Just salt and pepper. You know, the usual suspects."

"Do you girls have everything you need tonight?" Aunt Vicky asked. "Toothbrushes, toothpaste? Pajamas?"

Sam said nothing, knowing that Caitlin would answer.

"We have all that stuff," Caitlin said, on cue.

Her sister did not say that it was their caseworker, Mrs. Washington, who had given the supplies to them—brand-new brushes and floss and shampoo tucked into brand-new toiletry bags, pink for Caitlin and green for Sam. The implication had been clear: they were going to be away from home long enough to need these things. Longer than one night. Longer than two. And now they'd been away so long that the little bottles of shampoo were almost empty. But Sam refused to ask Aunt Vicky or Hannah for more. What if they gave her a full-sized bottle?

"Good," Hannah said. "I'll be gone in the morning. I work in town. But your aunt Vicky and her business partner will be here working all day. You can ask for anything you need. Right, Vic?"

Aunt Vicky blushed red. Was she upset? Sam felt her heart shifting back into rabbit mode.

But Aunt Vicky only nodded. "Armen and I will be working here at the table. We have a project due, and I couldn't push the deadline. But if you girls need anything, just ask. Don't worry about interrupting."

Sam dug her fork into her eggs and silently vowed not to interrupt.

"Armen's son usually walks over with him during the summer, so don't be surprised if you see a scruffy-looking boy running through the yard," Hannah added.

Caitlin's eyes widened with interest.

"He's your age, Sam," Hannah continued, and Caitlin's excitement faded instantly. "We'll have more time to talk tomorrow about . . . everything," Hannah said. "You're both registered for school, but it doesn't start for almost three weeks. That should give us some time to get your supplies and whatever clothes—"

"School starts in two weeks back home," Sam said. "It starts on the twenty-eighth." Her own voice startled her.

It seemed to startle everyone else, too. Even the forks and knives stopped their clattering. Sam tried to melt into her chair, to become one with the wood.

"Sam," Caitlin hissed.

"No, it's okay," Hannah said smoothly. "Sam, honey, your caseworkers have asked us to proceed as if you'll be staying with us for . . . well, for a while. And that means school here, instead of Los Angeles. I know it's a shock, but we'll do our best to help. Okay?"

Sam did not answer, even though she felt Caitlin looking at her. How could she? How was this, in any way, okay?

"She'll be fine," Caitlin said quickly. She never let silences go too long. "Maybe she's just not used to being eleven yet." Caitlin bumped Sam's shoulder playfully, but the tiny display of sisterly concern was more for Aunt Vicky and Hannah's benefit.

"It seems like a good time for cake!" Aunt Vicky pushed away from the table abruptly, her chair scraping across the floorboards, and said, "I'll take your plates." She took Sam's before Sam had even finished with her eggs and replaced it with a clean one, and a fork.

"It's birthday cake," Aunt Vicky said, and there seemed to be a nervous question hidden in her words. "For your birthday."

Sam nodded dully. She clung to her chair as if a river had rushed into the room and was trying to sweep her away.

School was starting in two weeks. What would BriAnn think if Sam wasn't back by then? What would everyone say? Would all her classmates sit around at lunch talking about why she wasn't there?

Aunt Vicky plunked a glistening cake onto the table. The flames of eleven tiny candles bobbed and swayed atop the swirly chocolate icing.

"That looks amazing," Caitlin said, nudging Sam with her good elbow. "Doesn't it look good, Sam? You love chocolate!"

Sam gripped the seat of her chair even harder. Her voice had vanished. She couldn't have answered even if she'd wanted to. She managed to give Aunt Vicky a small smile.

"Make a wish," her aunt said, encouraged. "But don't tell us what it is, so it has a better chance of coming true."

Make a wish, and keep it to herself. Finally, a thing Sam could do!

She blew out the candles. Every last one.

Aunt Vicky cut the cake and put a huge slice on Sam's plate. The moment Sam tasted it, the tightness in her throat began to loosen. The cake was still warm from the oven. The gooey frosting soaked into the sponge and made it super moist. At home, she always heated hers up in the microwave, but it was never as good as this. She would have had a second piece if anyone had offered. No one did. Aunt Vicky slid the cake under a glass dome and collected their plates a second time.

"You girls can watch TV tonight," Hannah said. "And we have a few movies on DVD." Sam noticed that she didn't mention anything about school or Los Angeles again. Not that Sam could stop thinking about them anyway.

"Or we could play a game," Aunt Vicky added. "I have—"

"Can I use the treadmill in my room?" Caitlin interrupted. "I haven't gotten in a run in ages." She hefted her broken arm as proof.

"The doctor's instructions said light exercise was fine, so keep it at a jog," Hannah said. She chuckled. "I can't remember the last time I used that thing, so you'll probably need to dust it first. I'll grab the cleaning supplies."

And then Hannah and Caitlin were gone, off to the treadmill in Caitlin's room, leaving Sam alone in the kitchen with Aunt Vicky. Any second now, Aunt Vicky would speak. She would *ask Sam a question.*

And answering questions was the last thing Sam wanted to do. That's how she'd ended up in Oregon, after all. Because she'd been tired and confused when people had started asking her the sorts of questions that no one had ever asked before. She should have kept her mouth shut. *And now school was about to start, and Sam was in the wrong state.*

Sam pushed away from the table too quickly, sending her empty glass of milk into a wobbly dance, and hurried back to the room she'd been given. As she was closing the door, she heard Hannah say, "Where did she go?"

Away. To her books. To her *castle.*

The door to her room had a lock. Would Aunt Vicky get angry if she used it? She could get caught once, probably. She almost always got by at least once. The tiny switch fought her at first, but with a little force, the mechanism creaked and whined and the bolt slid into place.

Locked. Safe.

She pulled the sheets off the bed and dragged them into

the castle fort. Why would she sleep all exposed when she could have the walls of her fortress to protect her? Why all beds weren't fortified and defensible was a mystery. Rapunzel may have been trapped all the way up in that tower of hers, but she was probably sleeping better than everyone else in the kingdom. If Sam were Rapunzel, she would have cut her hair off and made sure no one could visit her at all.

As long as the tower was filled with books, of course.

Once her castle nest was *cozified*—which should totally be a real word—Sam crawled inside and cocooned herself in sheets. She surveyed the neat row of spines in her makeshift library, trying to decide which book to read. Her eyes kept going to her birthday present instead. To the worn box holding Fox & Squirrels.

She picked it up, and the title sparkled in her palm.

She opened it, and the cards warmed to her touch.

Sam woke with a start, a sweaty playing card still clutched in one hand. The Queen of Walnuts. One of its corners was freshly bent. Sam's heart began to pound as she pressed it back into place, tried to will away the crease. No luck. It was permanently ruined. How could she be so careless! What would Aunt Vicky do when she saw that Sam had already damaged the game?

"It's only a queen," said a voice. A *male* voice, but higher pitched than Sam's father's.

Sam's heart did not rabbit; it stopped completely. "Who's there?"

"I'm here," the voice said. "Crawl out of that horrid little cave you've made yourself, and I can introduce myself more properly."

"But I locked the door." It was all Sam could think of to say. "I shut the door, and I locked it."

"Yes, yes, those are the facts," the voice said. "But I am rarely concerned with such things. So predictable! Where's the fun? And besides, the window was wide open."

Sam couldn't breathe. No air would enter or exit her lungs. She was a stone statue of a girl. Someone would find her eventually and label her GIRL TOO TERRIFIED TO MOVE.

A face appeared in the opening of the castle fort.

The face of a fox.

The face of *the* fox.

He wore a hat, just like from the game, and a fancy coat, too. The fur on his face was a ruddy reddish brown until it reached the opening of his mouth, and it was silvery white below that.

"Fox got your tongue?" the fox asked.

The Girl of Stone did not blink.

The fox leaned against the wall of her fort, legs crossed, and picked at one of his claws. "I get this a lot, you know. The surprise. The shock. I'm a dashing fellow, and I fully understand your awe. Who wouldn't be awed by the sight of me?"

Sam raised an eyebrow. Terrifying foxes were one thing; arrogant ones were quite another.

"You're not real," she said. "I'm dreaming."

"You are not," the fox replied easily. "If you were dreaming, I would be much taller. I've always wanted to be ten feet at the shoulder. Give those ridiculous bears a run for their money. '*We're so big and scary, us bears. Rarr this, and Rarr that.*'" He mimicked a bear, claws out, and Sam couldn't help herself. She laughed.

The fox beamed. "There's our girl!"

It should have been scary, to see a fox smile. There were the fangs, of course, but all the teeth were sharp, not just those. And yet the fox's smile was . . . *charming*.

"I'm Ashander," the fox said. "And you are Samantha. We have similar names, by which I mean they are both composed of three syllables and an overabundance of vowels."

"Ashander," Sam said, testing it out. "I didn't know foxes had names like that."

"We don't *all* have names like that," Ashander said. "How confusing would that be? Someone would call one of us, and all of us would turn our heads. Imagine! And it would make taking roll in class a ridiculous endeavor."

"Foxes go to school?" Sam pictured it, row after row of foxes all sitting at their desks.

Ashander tsked. "Of course not! Foxes don't need school. We know everything already."

For a brief moment, Sam had forgotten how far she was

from her parents and her home. The talk of school reminded her. It was like getting splashed in the face with a bucket of sadness.

"Now that's a frown for the ages," Ashander said. "A veritably *prodigious* frown. What could cause such a thing?"

"I want to go back home to Los Angeles," Sam blurted. "School's starting soon, and all my friends will be wondering where I am, and—"

"Just a minute." The fox tilted his head, thinking. Somehow it made him even more handsome.

Sam's mood brightened. She didn't know how to get back home, but maybe the fox did!

"Quests are often about finding one's way home," Ashander said finally. "Dorothy in *The Wizard of Oz* wants to return to Kansas. Odysseus spends ten years trying to get back to his home in *The Odyssey*. And of course everyone knows the story about Justicus the bat and her epic flight home after the Battle at Sky Mountain."

"Um . . . ," Sam said, not wanting to admit that she'd never even heard of Justicus but also wanting very much for Ashander to tell her that story.

"Pishposh," Ashander said. "You know the story, you just don't remember knowing it. But the point remains: you want to return to your parents and your home. All great heroes do. That said . . . your particular request sounds almost impossible."

Sam crumpled.

"Oh, don't give up so easily," the fox said. "I said *almost impossible*, which is another way of saying *possible . . . just very hard*." He brought his furry face close to Sam's. She could have counted the whiskers on his cheeks. "Have you ever heard of . . . *the Golden Acorn*?"

A chill raced up Sam's back. She shook her head.

"It is a legendary artifact of incredible power," Ashander said, almost purring. Sam hadn't known foxes could even do that. "With the Golden Acorn in your paw, any wish you make will come true."

"Any wish?" Sam sat up a little taller. She could be back in Los Angeles, before *that night*. Before everything went wrong. In fact, she'd made that very wish earlier that night, when she'd blown out the candles on her cake.

"Yes, any wish. I wouldn't have said it if it weren't true!"

"Where do I find it?" Sam asked. She'd go now. Right this minute. There wasn't a second to lose.

But Ashander leaned away, crossed his arms over his chest. "Oh, Sam. You don't *find* the jewel of the forest—you *earn* it. More specifically, you pass the tests. Every good hero must prove their worth, isn't that right?"

Sam glanced at her tiny collection of books. The characters inside those stories always fought for the things they wanted. They never gave up. They were brave, even when they were scared.

Sam wanted to be brave, too. Maybe if she'd been a little

braver, a little better, back in Los Angeles, she could have kept her family together.

"I'll do it," she said, determined to at least try. "I'll do anything you say."

Ashander smiled. "Excellent. I knew I could count on you. And since the Golden Acorn is at its most powerful under the light of a full moon, you'd better hurry!" He started for the window.

"But it's practically a full moon now!" Sam called out.

"Which means we haven't a moment to waste." Ashander hopped onto the windowsill with ridiculous ease. "The first test is trust. Come to the forest tomorrow and find my emissaries. They will give you the details." His eyes narrowed and he grew serious. "And remember: tell no one about our meeting, or about anything I've said."

"I won't. I promise," Sam said, putting a hand over her heart. That part would be easy. She was already an expert at secrets.

"There's a good girl," Ashander said, suddenly smiling. "Don't dawdle. Time is running out!"

And then he was gone. Out into the darkening night in a blur of red and purple, and the quickest flash of white teeth.

CHAPTER FOUR

WHEN SAM AWOKE the next morning, she was curled up on the pillow-strewn floor of her makeshift castle like a tiny forest animal. An animal that somehow had access to bedsheets and had managed to get one of its feet tangled in them.

The smallest of knocks echoed on the door. Sam bolted upright.

"Breakfast," Aunt Vicky said.

Sam expected to hear the doorknob rattle. Her mother always did that, the knock barely a precursor to the door swinging wide open. It didn't matter if Sam was studying or sleeping or even changing her clothes. A closed door was not a thing her mother could abide for even a few seconds.

And if Sam dared to lock it anyway . . . *Samantha never listens,* her mother would say at dinner. *I just don't know what I need to do to get through to her.*

I'll find a way, her father would answer.

Today there was no rattle, no scolding. Aunt Vicky moved

up the hall, knocked on Caitlin's door, and kept going. Same as she had done at dinner the night before.

Sam remembered to breathe.

She scooped her hair into a ponytail and dug a fresh T-shirt and pair of shorts out of her suitcase. There was definitely no point in unpacking it now that she was going home. As soon as the next full moon, if she could pass all of Ashander's tests in time.

But how much time was that?

The watch! Sam pulled a small pouch from her backpack and unzipped it carefully. Inside were her three best necklaces, a charm bracelet, and a watch with leather straps that her mother said was very expensive. *He's sorry. He wanted you to have this.* Most importantly, the face of the watch had a cutout that an itty-bitty moon was slowly traversing. Her watch showed the phases of the moon!

She wrapped the watch around her wrist and fastened it, nice and tight. Was this what the Knights of the Round Table felt like when they put on armor? Or what Joan of Arc had felt the first time she'd lifted her sword? Almost like she was ready for anything.

Sam took one more breath and left the safe confines of the room, taking great care to shut the door behind her, waiting for the satisfying *snikt* of the latch. The house was quiet, and her footsteps creaked over the old floorboards. Smiling Hannah had already left for work. The computer equipment on the kitchen table had expanded overnight so that there was barely any space to eat. Aunt Vicky sat in a chair by the empty fireplace, quietly crunching a bowl of cereal. It was so quiet, in fact, that Sam could hear birds chirping—*birds!*—outside the open kitchen window.

Caitlin hadn't come out of her room yet. In Sam's eagerness to leave, she hadn't waited to hear the click of Caitlin's door opening first. Rookie mistake, and one she never would have made at home in LA. But if she was quiet enough, she might be able to turn around and—

"Morning," Aunt Vicky said through a mouthful of what looked—and sounded—like oat flakes. "Grab some cereal, if you want. Armen and Lucas will be here soon. You don't drink coffee, right? That's not a thing kids do?"

Some kids drank coffee, but not Sam. When she'd stolen sips of her mother's, it had been bitter and disgusting.

"Chocolate milk?" she asked hopefully.

Aunt Vicky frowned. "No, sorry. Just regular milk. But I can put it on the list. Hannah's going shopping after work today. We can get all your favorites." She winced a little. "Well, maybe not all of them. But some of them. Chocolate milk, definitely."

"Thanks," Sam said. She stepped into the small kitchen area and tugged at a cupboard, searching for bowls and cereal and everything she needed for this conversation to be over.

"Just one cabinet to the left, yeah, that one," Aunt Vicky said. "I know the bowls don't match the rest of the decor—insomuch as there *is* a decor—but they have chickens on them. I'm a sucker for chickens."

Sam hid her smile. She'd been a guest in the house for less than one day, and yet this was a fact she would already bet her life on.

"Do you . . . want to meet the chickens?" Aunt Vicky asked. Her half-finished bowl of cereal sat in her lap.

Under normal circumstances, Sam's answer would have been an enthusiastic yes. Was there any other possible answer to the question of meeting chickens? But she had things to do today, and those things involved a fox and a forest and mysterious emissaries. There was no time for chickens.

"I was thinking I'd take a walk in the woods this morning," Sam said, trying to channel Caitlin's ease with adults. "But . . . maybe another time?"

"Of course," Aunt Vicky said. She seemed disappointed, and Sam felt a pang of guilt. "I've already fed them this morning, but you can visit them whenever you'd like. Lucas insists on checking for eggs, and I'm sure he'd love the help."

Lucas. Sam had forgotten about him. She did *not* want to meet a new person, particularly a boy, and extra particularly a boy named Lucas. Not that she had anything against the name in general; she was simply certain that it was attached to a person she would not like.

Her mother used to say, "Caitlin doesn't have trouble making friends. Can't you try to be more like her?" As if a person could just wish themselves to be something new. As if every person were some kind of magician born knowing the most powerful spell in the world.

Aunt Vicky deposited her bowl into the sink and sat down behind one of her computer monitors at the kitchen table. The light reflected off her nose and cheekbones and chin, and her eyes were instantly intense. Sam wondered if she looked like that when she was reading a book. Like the only truly real things were on the page—or on Aunt Vicky's screen—and everything else was an illusion. Sometimes it was a lot easier to live in a book than it was to live in the real world. Maybe Aunt Vicky felt like that with her computer, too.

Sam poured herself some cereal—passing tests was bound to be demanding work that required a good amount of fuel—and perched on the edge of one of the living room chairs while she ate. She had just shoveled a heaping spoon of raisin-y oats into her mouth when the front door burst open and a small man rushed in like a winter wind. He was the opposite of Aunt Vicky: short and thin with a wide smile, light brown skin, and long, dark hair falling past his shoulders. He didn't look old enough to be someone's father—or dressed nicely enough to be one, either—but a boy followed him inside. A boy who was not smiling at all.

"Good morning, Vickster! Good morning, Vickster's niece, whom I have not yet had the pleasure of meeting!" the man said. "I'm Armen, but you can call me Armen. Because that's my name." He laughed despite the fact that nothing he'd said was funny. "This is my son, Lucas, but you can call him 'Hey, you!' Unless he tells you not to. And then you should call him whatever he likes, since that's one of the many ways we try to respect each other's choices in our family. And in the world, too, now that I think about it." He turned to Aunt Vicky. "Ready to get to work? I brought fresh tea!"

"I have tea here," Aunt Vicky grumbled.

"Yes, but not tea of any worth," Armen said. "I know this. You know this. Now the children know this, too."

He tossed his messenger bag onto a kitchen chair and plopped down next to Aunt Vicky. Within seconds, his eyes reflected the glow of the computer screen, and they both started pointing and murmuring to each other.

Sam knew she should get going, but she found herself standing next to the strange boy named Lucas. He had knitting needles in his hands, and a bunch of multihued yarn, and was doing odd things with them.

Perhaps *knitting*.

"Say hello, Lucas," Armen called from the table without looking up.

"Hello," Lucas said, also without looking up.

They were definitely related.

Sam studied the boy. Unlike his father, his hair was short, buzzed close on the sides with a mop of a forelock in front, like a horse.

"You're staring," Lucas said, but unless he had invisible eyes on the top of his head, he could not possibly know that because he was still moving his knitting needles back and forth and looping yarn—now it was yellow—around his finger for some clearly nefarious purpose.

"What are you making?" Sam asked.

"Don't know yet," Lucas answered.

"That's ridiculous," she said before she could stop herself. "I mean, don't you have to know before you start? Isn't there a recipe or something?"

Finally, he looked up at her, his eyes brown and deep set under shaggy eyebrows. "I just like to knit," he said. "I like the way the yarn feels, and the way the colors change, and I like doing stuff with my hands. I don't like following patterns." He looked back down and looped another length of yarn. "That's what they're called, you know. *Patterns*. Not recipes."

Sam's cheeks burned. She should have known what they were called or said nothing. Now she'd made him angry. Three minutes after they'd met.

"Maybe I'll knit a fried egg next," Lucas said. "Then it can be a pattern *and* a recipe!" He grinned and his eyebrows shot up, releasing his eyes from their shadowy prison.

Not angry after all. Sam grinned back.

"Take your nonsense outside," Armen said. "Grown-ups are trying to grown-up in here!"

Sam stiffened and headed for the door immediately, before

Armen got more upset. Lucas tucked his knitting into his messenger bag—a smaller version of his father's and bright red. "He's kidding," Lucas called after her. "He doesn't try to be funny when he's actually mad."

Her hand was already on the doorknob leading out. Her heart rabbited. Who pretended to be mad as a joke?

"Don't you want to finish your food?" Lucas asked, pointing at her half-eaten breakfast on the edge of the table.

Sam shook her head once and pushed outside.

In Los Angeles, the hot, dry air would have wrapped itself around her immediately, like a welcoming hug. Instead, a small puff of cool wind brushed past her, mussed her hair, and kept moving. It was a breeze that had places to go, things to do.

That was fine with Sam, because so did she.

The house and the chicken coop were surrounded by a wild swirl of forest, as if they were nestled in the eye of a very green hurricane. Sam scanned the dense cluster of trunks, looking for a flash of red.

She heard someone coming up behind her.

"Want to look for eggs?" Lucas brushed past Sam's shoulder, heading toward the chicken coop. He seemed perfectly comfortable, taking a path he'd clearly taken dozens of times before.

"You go ahead," Sam said, taking a step in the other direction. "I want to check out the forest first."

"Oh, I'll come with you," Lucas said happily. "The eggs aren't going anywhere." He started for the trees.

Sam looked from the forest to Lucas and back again. This boy was going to ruin all her plans. What could she say? What could she do? There was no way the emissaries—whoever they were—were going to talk to her with Lucas hanging around, and she couldn't afford to lose any more time. She glanced at her watch and its little moon, almost full.

"You coming?" Lucas asked from the edge of the woods. He was already at the first tree.

Sam scrambled to catch up to him, shuffling through ideas in her head. She needed some way to get rid of Lucas that did not involve tying him to a tree with his own yarn. Mostly because the yarn didn't look that strong.

It was hard to see where the yard ended and the real forest began. Sam expected her arms to tingle when she crossed the threshold, as if she'd gone through some magical barrier. And in a way, they did. The treetops blocked out the morning sun, and the air grew ever so slightly cooler. A swift breeze carried the scent of moist earth and pine in its wake.

"The forest here is old, but not too old," Lucas said. "If it was really old, there wouldn't be much in the way of shrubs or brambles or saplings—the big trees would take all the sunlight and resources for themselves." He walked confidently through the trees and bushes and started pointing. "Dogwood, vine maple, Douglas hawthorn, manzanita. Ooh, there's some poison oak! You should avoid that if you can."

Poison oak! Lucas knew a lot of very useful things. Maybe

Sam wouldn't tie him to a tree just yet. She looked at the plant and tried to commit its unassuming leaves to memory.

"I learned about poison oak the hard way," Lucas said. "My dad got it all over his arms and legs, and I had to take care of him for a week! Have you heard the rhyme? *Leaves of three, let them be.* I made him repeat it a hundred times."

Sam got an idea. "What's that one?" she asked, pointing to dense bush with thorny leaves.

"Oregon grape," Lucas said. "But don't get too excited. The grapes taste terrible. Trust me. I learned that the hard way, too."

Sam's plan did not require her to eat anything. No, it required bravery of an entirely different sort. *Heroes do this kind of thing all the time*, she reminded herself. And before she could change her mind, she reached out and poked one of the thorny leaves with her fingertip. Hard.

"Ow!" she yelped. A big, bright drop of blood sat on her finger, glistening and red like a berry.

"That's a deep one." Lucas winced sympathetically. "Sorry, I should have warned you."

"It's okay," Sam said. "Do you think you could get me a Band-Aid? Blood makes me a little dizzy."

"Sure," Lucas said brightly. "The house is right there—"

"Not from Aunt Vicky's house!" Sam interjected. "I . . . I don't want her to worry. Maybe you could get one from your house?" She felt terrible for tricking him, but it had to be done.

Lucas rubbed his chin. "I guess that makes sense. My dad

said Vicky has been stressed out about you coming here. She'd probably freak if she saw you were hurt. But we live on the other side of the forest, so it might take me a few minutes to run over and back."

Why was Aunt Vicky stressed about Caitlin and Sam's visit? They knew how to stay out of the way. Sam didn't know why, but it bothered her.

"Thanks," Sam said. "That would be really nice of you. I'm just feeling kind of woozy."

She glanced at the red bubble on her fingertip, and her chest tightened.

Drops of blood on the table, on the carpet. Her mother's voice, panicked.

"Be right back, then!" Lucas said with a mock salute. He headed into the trees, his satchel bumping on his hip as he ran.

"I'll wait here," she called after Lucas, only she intended to do no such thing.

From the Rules for Fox & Squirrels

INSTRUCTIONS

Shuffle the Harvest deck and deal 10 cards to each player. Add the Fox cards to the remaining deck and shuffle again. Now the Fox is hidden!

Play your turn and gather your nuts, but know this:

The Fox is always watching.

The Fox is always waiting.

You never know when the Fox will appear.

Stay vigilant, brave squirrel!

CHAPTER FIVE

SAM SUCKED THE blood from her finger. Maybe not the most sanitary way to handle a cut, but better than wiping it on her clothes by accident. Or accidentally wiping it on *poison oak*.

Now that she was alone, the forest seemed eager to show her its true self. As she walked deeper into its embrace, branches rustled. Shadows reached up from the ground, looping dark tendrils around roots and pulling flowers into darkness. The sun tried to fight its way through the treetops but was thwarted by the dense canopy of green. Aunt Vicky's house disappeared behind her, lost to the tangle.

Forests were dangerous places for heroes. It was easy to get turned around. To get lost. To stumble into a dragon's lair. To slide down a hole and end up face-to-face with the Cheshire cat. Sam touched the rough bark of a tree. It felt solid. Sturdy. Entirely unlikely to start talking. Maybe this forest was only trees—normal, everyday trees without any magic at all.

In fact, maybe Sam had imagined meeting Ashander in

the first place. Maybe there was no such thing as the Golden Acorn, and maybe school in Los Angeles would start without her. Maybe BriAnn would make new friends, and she'd draw all over their envelopes when she wrote them letters instead of writing to Sam.

Ugh. Sam hugged her arms to her chest and scanned the forest. Ashander had to be real. His emissaries had to be out here. She would find them, and she would find the Golden Acorn, and soon she'd be falling asleep in front of some boring old movie while her parents ate popcorn on the sofa behind her. Caitlin could play softball once her arm healed, and BriAnn would absolutely *not* have to make any new friends.

Sam had not lost everything. Not yet. Not when she still had a chance to save her family and her old life by being a little bit brave.

"Hello?" she said. The trees seemed to eat up her voice. She tried again, determined to be louder. "Is anyone there? Ashander sent me!"

There! A flash of blue!

"I see you by the tree!" she said, and then realized how ridiculous that sounded in a forest *made* of trees.

Something flew at Sam's face, and she did not duck in time. A small pebble hit her squarely between the eyes. It didn't hurt, but it was still plenty surprising.

"Hey!" she yelled, rubbing her forehead.

"Sorry, sorry, sorry!" A gray squirrel jumped up on a root—a gray squirrel wearing a bright-yellow tunic and tiny squirrel pants. "My aim is usually not that good. I must have *really* wanted to hit you."

"You got lucky," a second squirrel said. She was larger and brown, and wearing a shiny knight's helmet with the visor up. A sharpened twig hung like a sword from her belt. "I'm Birch, and that's Cedar. And if I had hit you with the stone, it would have been on purpose." She bowed briskly. Cedar, the squirrel in yellow, hastily followed her lead.

"And I'm Maple," said a third squirrel, coming out from behind a tree trunk. She wore a blue dress and a long blue scarf that rustled around her neck. Maple was clearly a Very Fancy Squirrel. And Very Serious. And seemed Very Much in Charge. "If you are, indeed, looking for Ashander's emissaries, then you have found them." She curtsied.

Sam did not know whether to curtsy or bow in return, and more important, she didn't know *how*. In the end, she went with a half-hearted salute and said, "I'm Sam. Samantha. Just Sam." Well, that was awkward. "Ashander said you would give me my first test."

"And so we shall," Maple said. "Come closer."

Sam crossed the distance until she practically towered over the squirrels.

"Not like that. Kneel before us, please," Maple said, shaking her head. "Honestly, are you sure Ashander sent you?"

"I'm sure," Sam said, setting her jaw. She clumsily knelt before the squirrels, her knees sinking into the cool earth. Rocks and roots pressed into her shins, but she was determined not to squirm.

Maple stood in the middle, her spine straight, her tail a floofy cloud behind her head. Birch stood to her right, brandishing her stick sword, and Cedar stood to her left, juggling pebbles.

The emissaries weren't exactly formidable—even Birch was barely a foot tall on her hind legs—but it was clear they *wanted* to be. Sam tried to look appropriately awed. She wished BriAnn were here with her sketchbook. BriAnn was always drawing trees and animals and bowls of fruit. She'd have squealed the minute she saw *talking squirrels wearing clothes*.

"Before we give you your clue, there are things you should know," Maple said. "Once you start a quest for Ashander the Fox, you must finish it. Giving up in the middle is not an option."

"I won't give up," Sam said immediately. "I need the Golden Acorn to get home."

"A noble cause!" Birch said, waving her sword. "I approve."

Cedar rolled his eyes but did not stop juggling.

"That's wonderful to hear," Maple said with a relieved sigh. "I'm sure everything will work out fine, then." Softer she repeated, "Yes, I'm sure everything will be just fine."

A shadow passed over Maple's face, and Sam recognized the pinched look in the squirrel's eyes. When a breeze swished through the woods, Maple shivered. Except it was late summer and not actually cold at all.

All of a sudden, Sam wanted to hug Maple. To pull her in, cradle the Very Proper squirrel against her chest and keep her safe. But she didn't know Maple well yet, and she certainly didn't know how to suggest such a familiar thing.

Maple smoothed the lines of her pretty blue dress and recovered her composure. "Very well, then. Birch, Cedar—Cedar, stop that juggling at once."

Cedar let two of the stones he'd been juggling drop to the ground and caught the last one on his nose. He twirled, bounced it off his feet like a soccer ball, and then sent it to rest with the others. Sam almost clapped. Birch sighed.

Maple returned her focus to Sam. "Are you ready for the riddle, Sam? We will only say it once."

The first test was a riddle! Like Gollum and Bilbo battled with in *The Hobbit*! Like the monstrous Greek sphinx used to ask its victims! Only, hopefully Sam wouldn't be eaten if she got the answer wrong.

"I'm ready," she told Maple solemnly, and held her breath. The entire forest seemed to join her. The birds stopped chirping, the branches stopped rustling. Even the wind paused to listen.

Maple raised her paw, and all three squirrels spoke in eerie unison. Their hushed voices echoed through the forest far louder than they should have, as if some ancient magic was amplifying them.

The Hunter asks for you to prey
on shadows twitching tails of gray.
In the bramble,
squeak and scramble,
snap the trap and make it swift!
Earn his trust with this small gift.

Sam shivered, partly from excitement and partly from the sense that something wildly dangerous had just begun. She immediately repeated the whole riddle to herself three times in order to memorize it. Only once she was satisfied that she knew the whole thing did she allow herself to consider what it might mean.

"The Hunter must be Ashander," Sam muttered to herself. "And the physical descriptions—twitching tails, squeak, scramble—they all make me think of an animal."

She glanced at the squirrels, hoping to see a sign of approval. Birch hopped from one foot to the other. Cedar clapped both his front paws over his mouth. Maple merely studied Sam and waited.

"Probably some sort of critter or rodent that can be found in brambles," Sam said. She decided to press her luck. "And they're often captured with traps . . . Is it a mouse?"

"No cheating!" Cedar scolded through his paws, his voice muffled. "It's against the rules."

"We can't help you," Birch amended. "Because it's not *honorable*."

"Because Ashander has forbidden it," Maple said solemnly. "That's the most important reason of all."

"I'm thinking out loud, not trying to cheat!" Sam said quickly.

"Most people think with their heads, not with their mouths," Maple chided. "And besides, the riddle tells you what you need to do. We're merely emissaries."

"So I need to somehow find a mouse and deliver it to Ashander," Sam said. That didn't sound too bad for a first test—

Wait.

Foxes *ate* mice.

The riddle used the words *hunter* and *prey*, which definitely implied that eating would be taking place. Was Sam really supposed to catch a real, living mouse and give it to Ashander as a snack? Could she actually do that?

"But if I bring it to him, will he eat it? In front of me?" Sam asked. The more she imagined it, the more upsetting it was.

"Tests are supposed to be difficult," Cedar said. He'd picked up his pebbles and was juggling again. "If they were easy, they wouldn't be tests."

Birch raised her sword. "You can do it, Sam! I believe in you!"

Sam smiled gratefully at the squirrel. But she wasn't so certain.

"You're on the path now," Maple said. "You accepted the quest and promised Ashander. You must follow through." She took Sam's hand in two paws. "Rules can change all the time, but not that one. Never that one."

Maple's nose twitched. She sniffed the air.

"The boy is returning. We must go." She released Sam's hand but not before patting it one last time. "Do what you must do. It's the only way to get to the Golden Acorn. It's the only way to make things right."

Sam sniffed the air but smelled only soil and pine, with a mix of flowers. When she turned back to the squirrels, they had already disappeared. Only Cedar's tiny pile of juggling rocks remained, and a message Birch had carved into the earth with her twig sword.

It said: HURRY.

Chapter Six

"*SAM? WHERE ARE you?*" Lucas called.

Sam stood and brushed the forest from her knees. The stones left little divots in her skin, like they didn't want to be so easily forgotten. "Over here," she called, and he appeared almost immediately, his cheeks red from running.

"Sam! You're okay!"

"Of course I'm okay," she said. Was he really worried about her? "It was only a small cut."

"Yeah, but there are other dangers in the woods," Lucas said. "Ravines. Pits. Rusty nails. Old boots."

"Some of those aren't dangers," she said, laughing. "Some of those are just *things*."

"Say that after you've tripped over a boot. Oh!" He held out his hand. "Here's a Band-Aid for your finger."

Sam took it, suddenly embarrassed that she'd asked him to go to so much effort. He'd done it without complaining, even though they'd just met. She put the Band-Aid over the pinprick on her finger and tucked the wrapper into her pocket.

"Thanks," she said, and meant it. "That helps."

"I brought you something else, too," Lucas said. He rummaged through his satchel and pulled out a battered brass disk. "It's a compass! I got a new one for my birthday in March—it does a lot more things—so I don't need this one anymore." He pressed a button on the top and the lid flipped open. Inside she saw *N*, *E*, *S*, and *W* labeled around a circle, with a jittery arrow pointing left. "Do you know how to use one?" he asked.

"No, but I can figure it out," she said, certain she could. There'd simply been no need for compasses in Los Angeles, where all the streets were marked with signs and there was no possible way to get lost in the trees. Mostly because there were so few trees.

"Okay, cool," Lucas said. "My dad says I'm not allowed to explain things if someone says they don't want to hear, but I do know a lot about compasses, in case you change your mind. My dad and I go camping all the time, and I'm always in charge of the map." He reached into his bag again and retrieved his knitting. Maybe he always needed to be doing something with his hands. Like BriAnn and her sketching. Sam thought guiltily about the unanswered letter that was tucked into her backpack. She would write back as soon as she had a chance . . . and as soon as she figured out what to say. But for now, she needed to focus.

The compass sat in Sam's palm, cool and heavy, like some sort of talisman. She twisted it left and right but the arrow stayed steady, as if it were anchored by an invisible string.

"It always points north," Lucas said, craning his neck to see. "So to walk north, you turn in place until the *N* lines up with the arrow."

"You're *still* talking about the compass," Sam said, but she spun until the arrow and *N* were touching anyway, and peered into the forest. North looked just like all the other directions. Without the compass, she never would have known it was there.

Lucas knew a lot of things that Sam didn't. Maybe she could get him to help with her quest if she didn't give him any of the details. She'd have to be careful not to betray Ashander's confidence.

"Do you see a lot of *mice* when you go camping?" she asked lightly.

"Mice? Sure," he said. "And deer and owls, and even one time a coyote. The coyote was my favorite."

"A coyote! I've never seen a coyote at all," Sam said. "And I've never gone camping, either. My mom hates bugs. Does your mom go with you and your dad?"

"Nope," Lucas said. "I've never even met my mom."

Sam glanced at Lucas. She shouldn't have asked. She should have known better. It was none of her business.

"Don't make that face," Lucas said.

"What face?"

He furrowed his brow and squeezed his mouth into a tinier version of itself.

"I do not look like that!" she said, trying to smooth out her forehead and unclench her mouth.

"You do a little," Lucas answered with a grin. "It's okay. I've never met my mom, but my dad told me a lot about her. She lives in New York City and works for a fancy magazine and does not have any pets, not even a fish or a rabbit or a snake."

Sam had so many questions, none of which felt appropriate to ask. What was it like to grow up without a mother? What was it like to know that she was living somewhere else and didn't want to be with Lucas or his father? What was it like to be so far away from one of your parents?

Maybe she already knew the answer to that last one.

Lucas picked up an acorn from the forest floor and tossed it deeper into the woods. "You and your sister and your aunts should come camping with us sometime," he said.

"That's not—"

"You'd need your own tent, but we have an extra canoe and a bunch of life vests if we go to the lake."

Talking to Lucas was like trying to drink water from the yard hose—there was too much all at once.

"We can't go camping," Sam interrupted. "We're not going to be here that long. We're just staying a few days, and then we're going back to Los Angeles. School starts on the twenty-eighth."

Whatever she said—it was all just the truth—seemed to surprise Lucas. "That's not what my dad told me. He said you're staying here for good."

"That's not true." Sam's cheeks grew hot. "Why would he say that?"

"Didn't your dad hurt your sister?" Lucas asked, furrowing his brow. "They won't let you go back. Probably not ever."

Sam stood in front of Lucas, frozen, her brain refusing to tell her what to say or do. No one had ever said those words aloud before. Not Mrs. Washington, not the doctors, not her mother. Not even Caitlin. It was wrong to say them. *Wrong.* She didn't have to listen. *She wouldn't.*

She wanted to tell him to go away. She wanted to *scream.* But her mouth would not open, the words would not come. Sam closed her eyes and breathed. Her heart beat, too, and although it was fast, it wasn't rabbiting. Anger was not the same thing as panic. Panic was a feeling trapped inside the chest, a bird beating its wings inside its cage. Anger was when feelings made it past the bars. When they made it out.

The compass sat in her palm, heavy and warm, and suddenly Sam wanted to throw it. To throw it *at him.*

The thud against the wall of Caitlin's room. Glass shattering. A muffled cry.

Sam pulled back her arm and, at the last second, threw the compass at Lucas's feet. He yelped and jumped back as if she had hit him. As if she'd thrown a bomb instead of a small metal object.

When Sam saw Lucas's shocked expression, her anger vanished as quickly as it had appeared, replaced with the deepest, hungriest shame that gobbled her up from the inside.

It was not good to be angry. Anger was a disease, spreading from one person to the next. Sam could come home from school angry, like when Braydon Mannon stole her book—she'd been reading *The Westing Game* and Turtle was so close to solving the big mystery—and he wouldn't give it back for the whole ride and on top of that lost her place. She'd bring the anger into the house and lash out at Caitlin or her mother, and her mother would get infected next, her lips thinning into a line. If she was still angry when Sam's father got home, then that was it. He was always halfway there already. Her mother's anger would push him over and then dinner would be lectures or yelling or . . . worse.

The forest was dangerous after all. *Far too dangerous.*

Sam turned and ran. She headed back to the house, because she didn't know where else to go. She had no refuge. No sanctuary. She couldn't crawl under the covers of her own bed and read by the light of a flashlight, like she had done so very many times before.

Lucas should not have said those horrible things.

He should *not*.

But she shouldn't have thrown something at him, either. Not even at his feet.

Aunt Vicky's house appeared through the trees, and even though it wasn't home, Sam was relieved to see it. All she needed was some time to herself. First to catch her breath, and then to figure out how to catch a mouse. Lucas had distracted her from her quest, and she wouldn't let it happen again.

The quest was the only thing that mattered.

As soon as she opened the door to the kitchen, she realized her mistake.

Armen and Aunt Vicky were right there, right in front of her, still working at the table surrounded by that morass of cords and computer equipment.

"Vickster's niece, whose name I have since learned is Samantha, you have returned!" Armen said.

Sam stood in the doorway, uncertain how to answer such a strange greeting.

"Hi, Sam," Aunt Vicky added in her quiet voice.

"Ooh, there's the culprit," Armen said, pointing at the computer screen. "That equation is not doing what it's supposed to do."

Aunt Vicky slid the computer mouse across the mouse pad and double-clicked. Her fingers flew over the keyboard, filling the kitchen with soft percussion.

"My son has not run off to join the wolves, I hope," Armen said, not taking his eyes off the screen. "He does that sometimes for fun, but I don't like it even then."

"No," Sam answered. And then, afraid he might continue the conversation, she added, "He's, um, fine."

"Excellent," Armen said. "What every parent likes to hear."

Aunt Vicky clicked the mouse again, and both she and Armen watched the screen as if it were the most exciting movie in the world. A second later, they cheered.

"Yes!" Aunt Vicky said.

"This calls for cake!" Armen answered.

Aunt Vicky laughed. "It's not even eleven yet."

"Pre-lunch cake is the best cake," Armen answered. "Right, Samantha?"

Sam did not want cake. She'd lost her appetite in the woods, and every time she thought about catching a real, live mouse and giving it to Ashander, her stomach twisted a little more.

But she couldn't say any of that, so she looked longingly down the hallway toward her room and said, "Sure."

"I'll get the plates," Aunt Vicky said. She pushed the computer keyboard from the edge of the table and shoved the mouse back into the little thicket of cords.

A *thicket* of cords.

Sam barely noticed as Armen and Aunt Vicky bustled around her.

A *thicket* was like a *bramble*.

She couldn't stop staring at the computer mouse.

A mouse.

With a computer-cord tail.

That sort of squeaked and scurried when it was used, didn't it?

Sam's whole body buzzed with energy. It did this whenever she figured out the answer to a crossword puzzle with her dad, or when she and BriAnn designed a really cool new superhero.

The riddle told her to fetch a mouse, but it didn't say what *kind* of mouse. She could bring Ashander the computer mouse and pass the test without having to hurt anything or anybody.

Aunt Vicky held out a piece of cake on a plate. "Sam? Do you want milk?"

Sam took the plate and nodded. Her buzz faded.

She could give Ashander the computer mouse. But first, she had to steal it from Aunt Vicky.

From the Rules for Fox & Squirrels

INSTRUCTIONS

If, on your turn, you pull a Fox from the Harvest deck, forget about collecting nuts. None of the cards you've already played will count toward your score, and you cannot play new cards at all. You must focus instead on earning the Fox's favor. NOTHING ELSE MATTERS UNTIL YOU DO.

 Do not attempt to deceive the Fox.

 The Fox will know.

 The Fox ALWAYS *knows.*

CHAPTER SEVEN

SAM HAD NO opportunity to steal the mouse while they ate their "morning celebration cake." Aunt Vicky and Armen were always there, always hovering around the table or actively using the mouse. She didn't want to wait. Her prey was right there! But she had to be smart and patient, like a hunter. Like a fox.

"Sam, you don't have to stay in here with us. I know we're boring," Aunt Vicky said. "Do you want to go back outside?"

"No," Sam said quickly. She didn't want to face Lucas again. "Maybe Caitlin wants some cake. I'll take some to her."

She jumped up to cut another slice before anyone could object.

"Good idea," Aunt Vicky said. "I should have thought of that."

"Well, technically only the people in the vicinity of a victory deserve victory cake," Armen said, chasing the last of his cake crumbs with his fork. "But we can let it slide just this once."

Aunt Vicky poured a glass of milk and handed it to Sam. "For Caitlin. Thank you."

Sam took the milk in her non-cake-holding hand and scurried down the hallway, like a mouse escaping its doom.

A low hum emanated from Caitlin's room. Sam balanced the cake plate atop the glass and knocked. No answer. There never was, from Caitlin. Her earbuds blocked everything out.

Sam opened the door. Caitlin was on the treadmill, earbuds in her ears, eyes closed to the world, the rhythm of her feet hitting the belt like a steady heartbeat. Even with her arm in a cast, Caitlin had so much confidence. So much calm. Like she knew who she was all the time, instead of mostly just pretending.

Caitlin opened her eyes and saw Sam holding the cake. She raised an eyebrow and nodded to the nightstand.

There wasn't much space to walk. The treadmill took up almost half the room, and the bed ate up the other half. Even so, Caitlin had managed to strew clothes everywhere, as if the whole place was a combination of hamper and closet.

Sam deposited the milk and cake as directed and started to leave.

"Hey," Caitlin said. The treadmill whirred to a stop.

Sam turned at the doorway, startled. "Hey."

"So what's the boy like?" Caitlin asked. "Decent friend material? Maybe more-than-friend material? I want deets!" She stepped off the treadmill and downed the entire glass of milk.

"Lucas? He's okay," Sam said, but she could feel heat swarming to her cheeks. "I don't need any more friends."

Caitlin put the empty glass down and began shoveling cake

into her mouth. "Sure you do. Unless you have a whole bunch of secret Oregon friends I've never met before."

Sam almost told Caitlin about Ashander and the squirrels but remembered her promise. "Maybe I do."

Caitlin snorted. "Books don't count."

"They count to me," Sam said. She watched Caitlin eat another forkful of cake. "Don't you miss *your* friends? What about your teammates?"

"Sure," Caitlin said, and paused. "You know, I was going to pitch next season. Coach told me last year."

"Pitch!" Sam squealed. How could Caitlin have kept this a secret?

"That's right," Caitlin said, finishing off the last of her cake. "Maria Cortez transferred to a private school, and I've got the next best arm." She stared down at her arm, as if she'd forgotten it was in the cast. "Or, I *had* the next best arm, I guess."

"You will again," Sam assured her. What else had Caitlin been keeping from Sam?

Caitlin sighed. "Whatever. Maybe I don't even want to play softball anymore. It's something to think about anyway. All the choices we have now. You should start thinking, too." She flopped onto the bed, tucked her earbuds back into her ears, and pressed a button on her music player. Her eyes closed instantly and her head bobbed with music Sam couldn't hear.

Conversations with Caitlin often ended like this—abruptly, and before Sam realized they were over.

Back home, Sam would sometimes pull out a book and read on the floor of Caitlin's room. Sometimes Caitlin would kick her out when she noticed, and sometimes she wouldn't. It was nice to be in the same room, each of them doing their own thing but sort of doing it together.

There was absolutely nowhere to sit on the floor of Caitlin's current room. Not unless Sam wanted to fold up the treadmill or move Caitlin's clothes, and she knew better than to attempt either of those things. Instead, she snuck quietly into the hallway and into her own room.

Light shone through the window. The plastic bins of her castle fort were not entirely opaque, and the sun was doing its best to reveal the shadowy secrets inside each one. Sam itched to open them. She felt like a thief inside a vast chamber of gold and treasure who'd been told to touch nothing.

With a heroic effort, she sat inside the fort instead, pulled out her notebook, and wrote a letter to BriAnn. Or at least tried to.

What was she supposed to say?

When BriAnn came over after school or on weekends, she laughed when Sam's dad made a joke and chatted with Sam's mom about classes. BriAnn thought Sam's parents were *fun*, and around BriAnn, they were. But BriAnn had no idea what it was like all those other times, when no one else was watching.

Lucas's voice echoed in her head like some unbroken spell. *Didn't your dad hurt your sister? They won't let you go back. Probably not ever.*

Why wouldn't he shut up?

Sam tried to focus on her letter to BriAnn. Why wouldn't Sam be in LA when BriAnn got back from her cousin's wedding? Maybe her first idea—the one she'd had in the car on the way to Aunt Vicky's—was the best: that she'd been whisked away on a surprise trip to Hawaii with her whole family. It had been her mother's idea. Sam's mom was always leafing through travel magazines and ripping out articles like "The Ten Best Barbecues to Eat Poolside."

Sam had never actually been to Hawaii, but she'd seen plenty of ocean documentaries with her dad. It wasn't hard to build a fictional trip from those. *The ocean is so blue! I went snorkeling and saw a sea turtle! Oysters taste okay but look disgusting— like a pile of guts!* At least that was how Marcia Goodman had described eating an oyster in homeroom last spring. Sam hadn't appreciated the vivid description at the time, but she was grateful for it now!

It wasn't hard to fill up most of the page. She drew palm trees and coconuts in the margins. They looked more like misshapen flowers, so she labeled them in tiny print to be safe.

She signed her name in cursive, studied the page, and added one more line. *P.S. I'll be back before school starts.*

The words sat there on the page, simple and powerful, like a magic spell of her own.

Take that, Lucas.

She took a stamp from her pencil case—she always kept a

few there—but even after digging through her entire backpack, she couldn't find an envelope. Not a single one! Caitlin or Aunt Vicky might have one, but she didn't want to ask. What if they wanted to see the letter she'd written? What if they saw the palm trees?

No. Better to find one, if she could. There was a desk in this room, after all. Maybe it had been Aunt Vicky's office. Carefully, she slid open the drawers of the desk, one by one.

Pens and pencils. Rulers. Scissors, some with decorative edges like ones people used for scrapbooking and art class. Faded receipts so old the writing was wearing off. The bottom drawer, the biggest, was stuffed with user manuals. Big dull guides for using the coffee maker and the toaster oven and the rice cooker. No envelopes anywhere.

Of course, she could always check the bins.

They might be teeming with envelopes.

Sam pulled a plastic bin from the top of her castle fort and placed it on the floor in front of her. The bin's sides were milky-white plastic, but the lid almost sparkled, gemstone blue. She ran her hands over the smooth sides. She didn't have to open all the bins. Just a few. Just until she found an envelope. It wasn't such a terrible crime, not really. And no one would ever have to know.

But before she tugged at the lid—before she did anything, really—she stopped to make sure it was safe.

Voices carried easily in this house. Aunt Vicky and Armen

were still working at the kitchen table. Sam froze as she heard Lucas shuffling in and out of the house, the front door slapping closed each time, but she knew he wouldn't come into her room.

No one ever yelled at him for making so much noise. For not knowing if he wanted to be in or out and staying there. For asking for snacks. He interrupted his father twice for no better reason than to show him something he'd found—a tiny green chicken egg the first time, then a flower that smelled like grapefruit. Nonsense things . . . though she wouldn't have minded smelling the flower, just to see if he was right.

Sam could not imagine interrupting her own father like that. Not unless she could tell he was in a good mood, and probably not even then. Good moods could turn in a flash. Lightning could strike out of nowhere—even if there wasn't a cloud in the sky. You could never be sure what you were going to get. Some days it was exhausting. Some days, she was sloppy or tired and she made a mistake. Those were awful days. *You brought this on yourself.*

Sam found the sharp edge of the plastic lid with her fingers and tugged. The lid didn't budge. She pulled harder, but it was stubborn, gripping the bin with all its might. Finally, she yanked.

The lid flew off and clattered against the closed bedroom door. Sam winced, waiting for the footsteps that would surely come. The raised voices that would undoubtedly follow.

Rabbit heart. Rabbit heart. Rabbit rabbit rabbit.

In the kitchen, Armen laughed. Keyboards clacked.

No one came.

Eventually, Sam unclenched her body and peered inside, hoping for envelopes—or something better—and found, instead, a plain blue teddy bear. She poked its soft, adorable gut. It did not talk, or spew gems, or do anything even remotely interesting. Were all the bins full of stuffed animals?

She opened another and found cats: a tiny tiger with a big grin, a leopard with beanbag paws, a fluffy white Persian with a rhinestone collar and, inexplicably, a tiny eyepatch. The next one held a lone giraffe wearing a tiny scarf on its head and a plastic gold hoop attached to its ear. The fourth contained a shark and a starfish, both with goofy smiles and huge, anime eyes. The shark, like the Persian cat, wore an eyepatch. Had there been an epidemic of eye-gouging back when Aunt Vicky was a kid?

Sam wrenched the lid off another bin and found a small nest of stuffed squirrels, brown and gray, with big fluffy tails not unlike those that belonged to Maple, Birch, and Cedar. When she picked one of them up, a ring fell off its tail.

A real silver ring with a blue stone.

Blue was Sam's favorite color. She slipped the ring on one finger, then another, then another until . . . there. Perfect fit! She held out her hand and splayed her fingers, like her mother always did when trying on rings. The silver sparkled. The blue stone had little flecks of white mixed in. It was so pretty, it had to be magic. Would it help light her way to the Golden Acorn?

Out in the hallway, a door opened. Caitlin's door. Sam's heart barely had a chance to jump into rabbit mode before her own door swung open and Caitlin's head appeared.

"Hey, what kind of sandwich do you—*whoa.*" Caitlin gaped at the open bins arrayed around Sam like the debris from a bomb. "What are you doing? That's not your stuff."

Sam scrambled to put the lids back on the bins. "It's nothing. I'm not doing anything."

"Yeah, right," Caitlin said. "Those are Aunt Vicky's things."

"It was an accident," Sam blurted. Which made no sense. But she always got like this when she got caught, always said the first thing that came into her head. *Always messed up.*

"Clean this up right now," Caitlin said. "Put everything back exactly the way it was. I'll keep Aunt Vicky distracted."

"I'll put everything back," Sam mumbled, snapping the last lid into place.

"Good," Caitlin said. "I don't know what you were thinking, Sam. Don't ruin this for us."

The door slammed shut, and Sam sat there, hands shaking.

She wasn't trying to ruin anything. She was trying to *fix* it.

If she could only tell Caitlin about Ashander. If she could only let her in on the plan, then Caitlin would understand. When Sam found the Golden Acorn, nothing that happened in Oregon would matter. They'd fly back to Los Angeles and live with their parents, and they'd never see Aunt Vicky or Hannah or Lucas again. This place was a dream—a nightmare—and Sam was the only one fighting to wake up.

Sam folded her letter to BriAnn and shoved it deep into her notebook so no one would find it. The silver ring with its pretty blue stone glinted from her finger. No one had been missing it. Maybe it was okay if she wore it just a little longer. She could put it back in the bin later, before she went home.

CHAPTER EIGHT

SAM INTENDED TO stay in her room for the rest of the day, but as soon as she was done putting all the bins back in place, Birch appeared on the windowsill.

"It's far too nice a day to sit inside," the squirrel said. "Come outside with me!"

"But Lucas is out there," Sam said with a scowl.

"The forest is vast and he is only one person," Birch countered. "Are you a hero or not?" She puffed out her furry white chest and raised her stick sword. "To the trees. Adventure awaits!"

Then Birch leaped off the window and galloped on all fours across the yard. When the squirrel got to the first line of trees, she turned back and beckoned to Sam.

Well, there was no getting out of it now!

Sam slunk out of her room and past Aunt Vicky and Armen in the kitchen, mumbling something about getting fresh air as she stepped outside. Aunt Vicky's voice followed her, but only to say, "Have fun!"

Sam saw Lucas sitting by the chickens, seemingly absorbed in his knitting. She tiptoed in the other direction, doing her best ninja impersonation. Halfway across the yard, she felt a sneeze coming on. The mighty hero, betrayed by pollen! She pinched her upper lip with her fingers like BriAnn had showed her once, and managed to stuff down the sneeze. Lucas, who had surely been about to look up and discover her, remained oblivious.

Disaster averted!

"Over here," Birch called, waving her sword from the shade of a massive tree.

Sam made a shushing motion, then hurried the rest of the way until she reached the cover of the tree's branches. Immediately, spots of sunlight danced all over her.

"Nature's disco ball!" Sam grinned. "I bet the fairies in the forest throw fantastic parties."

Birch huffed. "I wouldn't know. They never invite me."

"You mean there are actually fairies? For real?" Sam wasn't sure why she was surprised, considering she was talking to a squirrel in a suit of armor.

"Of course they're real! Follow me. I'll prove it," Birch said, and bounded deeper into the woods. Sam spared another glance at the house, then headed after Birch.

Birch wove through the trees and eventually led Sam to a small grassy patch protected by three slender pines. Dozens of white-capped mushrooms arranged in a perfect circle sprouted from the lush green. No regular, non-fairy mushrooms would ever have grown like that.

"A fairy circle," Sam breathed. "What do they use it for?"

"Oh, the usual," Birch said casually, as if she got asked about fairies every day. "They cast spells and curses. Hold naming ceremonies. Throw parties that they don't invite me to." She swiped her sword at one of the mushrooms—just not close enough to actually hit it.

Sam knelt for a closer look. Was it the sunlight, or were they sparkling just a little bit? "Where are the fairies now?"

"In the trees and underground, mostly," Birch said. "They've got warrens and nests just like the rest of us. Only, their magic hides the entrances from humans and other predators. From anyone they don't want interrupting their business."

"I wish I had that magic," Sam said wistfully. Then her bedroom could become a true haven, a place that no one could enter. *That no one could even see.*

"Oh, who needs fairies? Dance with me!" Birch leaped into the fairy circle and held out her paws. "Come on, we'll make our own party!"

Sam shook her head without thinking.

The fairies might get mad.

"Please?" Birch said, wringing her paws together. "No one ever wants to dance with me."

Sam studied the sad little squirrel in front of her. Maybe it was worth taking a few risks if it would make Birch happy.

"Ooh, do you hear that music?" Sam said. "It's one of my favorite songs!"

Birch cocked her head, twitched an ear.

Sam stepped into the center of the fairy circle, careful not to crush a single mushroom. "Do you hear it?" She twisted her hips in time with the imaginary rhythm.

"Oh, I get it. Yes, I hear it now!" Birch wiggled her tail to an entirely different rhythm. The disco-ball sun didn't seem to care, showering them both with glittery light.

Even as she danced, Sam peered into the forest, expecting Aunt Vicky or Caitlin or Lucas to appear. It was hard to do anything back home in Los Angeles without someone else seeing you. There were people everywhere, all the time. Even in their condo, no door was ever truly shut.

She didn't want anyone to see her and laugh at her for dancing. For believing in fairies. For befriending a squirrel.

But no one came. No one saw.

Sam breathed deep and twirled. There was only dappled sunlight and trees as far as her eye could see in every direction.

Birch twirled as well and they both spun faster and faster until they lost their balance and collapsed in a heap of squirrel and girl. Sam laughed harder than she had in a long time.

Maybe she didn't need fairy magic here, if she could come outside and get away. If she could be herself, without anyone watching.

By the time Sam made it back to the house, Lucas and Armen were gone and Hannah's car sat in the driveway. Hannah herself was inside the kitchen unloading groceries. Aunt Vicky chopped onions on a cutting board. Sam nodded at them and snuck back to her room, trailed by the smell of sizzling butter and herbs. Her stomach grumbled eagerly. Dancing was hard work, especially when you had to make up your own music.

She changed into a fresh T-shirt. As she was redoing her ponytail, her door opened suddenly.

"Looks good in here," Caitlin said, assessing the room. She nodded to Sam's suitcase. "Now you just need to unpack."

"No," Sam said, irritated, even though she had just been thinking it might be time to hang up some of her clothes. "I'll just have to pack it again."

"So then you'll pack again," Caitlin said, like it was no big deal. She took a step into the room. "It's not bad in here. Nice view of the trees. Decent space once these bins are gone. Plenty of room for those nature posters you like."

"My posters are all back home, on the walls of my *real* room," Sam shot back. She thought of the fairy circle and the trees and all that green, but shook the image from her head.

Maybe it had been fairy magic, after all, trying to trick her into forgetting her quest.

Caitlin sighed. "Suit yourself, nerd. Time for dinner."

Sam followed her. Aunt Vicky motioned to the table, and Sam sat down, glancing quickly at the computer mouse, practically hidden in the cords. She forced herself to look away and focus on Aunt Vicky pouring milk into a tall glass and orange juice into a small one. Sam would have preferred her beverages the other way around, but didn't say so.

"It smells amazing," Caitlin said. "I'm so hungry!"

Hannah grinned. "Good thing, because I've made enough for an army."

"Did you get all those eggs from the chickens in the yard?" Caitlin asked. She was good at asking the sort of questions that adults loved to answer.

Aunt Vicky snorted. "They lay enough for *two* armies."

"Did you see any eggs when you went out with Lucas, Samantha?" Hannah asked.

Sam had just taken a big gulp of milk and choked a little in her rush to answer.

"She did," Caitlin answered, clapping Sam's back as she coughed. "She told me she saw three of them."

"They were really cool," Sam sputtered. She took another long drink of milk so no one would ask her any follow-up questions.

Something chirped. Aunt Vicky hopped up, pulled a phone out of her back pocket, and frowned when she saw the number.

"Excuse me, girls." She exchanged a quick look with Hannah, then strode out the front door to talk outside.

"Do you girls like sausage?" Hannah asked briskly. "I have meat and nonmeat options."

"Meat for me, nonmeat for Sam," Caitlin said. "That was so thoughtful to have both kinds."

"It was Vic's idea," Hannah said. "She's always thinking. It's one of the things I love about her."

She brought the pans over, one at a time, and scraped sausage and "sausage" onto their plates.

Aunt Vicky came back inside, her phone clutched in her hand. "We're going to have a visitor tomorrow. Mr. Sanchez from the state. He's going to see how you girls are doing. He'll ask a few questions, take a look around, maybe meet the chickens. Should be an easy visit." She offered Sam and Caitlin a quick smile but glanced at Hannah with worried eyes.

"Mr. Sanchez is very nice, girls. I'm sure you'll like him. What time will he be here?" Hannah asked, her voice still calm. She tossed the scrambled eggs in a huge pan, and none of them spilled. "I've got some hours saved. I can take off work."

Aunt Vicky's entire body seemed to relax. "Ten. That would be great. You don't have to do it. But it would be great."

"Of course I do," Hannah said, and squeezed Aunt Vicky's arm.

Aunt Vicky sat down again, but she was clearly distracted. She finished her orange juice in one gulp.

Unease filled the kitchen like smoke. Caitlin could sense it, too.

"How fun to have breakfast food for dinner," Caitlin said. "Do you do this a lot?"

Aunt Vicky's eyes came back from the faraway place they had gone. "Um ..."

Hannah piped up. "We both love breakfast, and we both hate rules that don't make sense. We prefer to make our own rules! I hope you girls are okay with that." She placed the big pan of eggs in the center of the table and took her seat.

"So we can have ice cream for dinner tomorrow?" Caitlin asked.

Hannah laughed. "Nice try, but I said *rules that don't make sense*. It makes sense to eat something healthy before filling up on sweets."

Aunt Vicky took a big spoon and started divvying up the eggs onto each plate. "There, um, may have been some mid-morning cake today."

"Oh, really!" Hannah said. "The truth comes out." She winked at Sam.

Caitlin dove into her eggs like a starving person. Sam blew on her eggs first, to make sure she didn't burn her mouth, and then ate her first bite thoughtfully. The butter made them silky and smooth. Little bits of green onion and broccoli added pops of crunch and flavor. Without thinking, she said, "Do you have any ketchup?"

Aunt Vicky jumped up from the table and grabbed it from

the fridge. "Here you go! I used to eat my scrambled eggs with ketchup, too."

Sam looked at the bottle for a moment, still surprised that she'd asked and that it seemed to be no big deal. She took it gingerly, made a little pool of ketchup on the side of her plate, and handed the bottle back. Aunt Vicky added two dots and a curvy line of ketchup to her own eggs. *A smiley face.* Sam grinned. Maybe she'd do that next time.

"How is your arm feeling?" Hannah asked Caitlin. "Is it itchy? The last time I had a cast, it itched constantly."

"It's not so bad." Caitlin touched her broken arm with her good hand. "But why did you have a cast?"

"I used to kayak," Hannah said. "Not the smart kind of kayaking, where you stick to lakes and slow-moving rivers. I would go to the coast and kayak in the ocean, sometimes in dangerous locations." The words were cautionary but her tone was . . . proud? "I tried to get into a cave once. Was racing high tide to do it. I barely made it back out before the entrance was sealed, and then only after I'd smashed my leg on the rocks."

"Cool!" Caitlin said.

Aunt Vicky shook her head. "Definitely *not* cool. It's a wonder that you made it to thirty at all."

"I'll drink to that," Hannah said, and held up her orange juice. "What, no one wants to drink with me?"

Aunt Vicky laughed and started to pour more OJ into Sam's

glass when Caitlin dropped hers. The glass shattered, flinging juice and bright shards in every direction. Sam watched, horrified, as tendrils of sticky liquid invaded Aunt Vicky's computer equipment and soaked into her keyboard.

The smell of butter and eggs hung heavily in the air. Outside, the birds were still singing in the trees, the chickens still clucking and scrabbling around the yard. But here at the table, time stood still. Sam couldn't move. She couldn't breathe. Caitlin had accidentally lobbed a grenade into their meal, and now they were holding their breath, waiting to see if it would explode.

"It's okay," Aunt Vicky said. She put the jug of orange juice on the table very carefully, as if she were approaching a frightened animal. "It's just a spill and some glass. An accident. No one is in trouble. It all cleans right up!" She paused, and her mouth seemed to fumble as she tried to find her next words. She spoke to them slowly. "Hannah and I are not angry."

"Of course we're not angry," Hannah said brightly. She moved freely, grabbing a sponge and dustpan, while the rest of them—Aunt Vicky, Caitlin, and Sam—were still immobilized.

"I'm sorry!" Caitlin jumped up. "I can help clean up."

"Why don't you gather the plates? There might be glass in some of them," Hannah said. "I can whip up a new batch of eggs."

Sam helped Caitlin clear the dishes, her body moving robotically even though, inside, her heart was still rabbiting. It didn't take long before every last sign of the broken glass was gone. Sam watched closely as Aunt Vicky wiped off the computer mouse and tucked it back into its nest of cords.

"Dinner, round two!" Hannah said, plopping a steaming pan of fresh scrambled eggs in the middle of the newly cleaned table. Aunt Vicky gave her a small, shaky smile.

Eventually, Sam's rabbit heart started to calm, and they finished their meal. Hannah did most of the talking, but Aunt Vicky and Caitlin jumped into the conversation, too. It was almost as if the whole glass-shattering incident had never even happened.

Afterward, when Caitlin asked to return to her room, Sam followed, feigning a yawn. Thankfully, it didn't take long for Hannah and Aunt Vicky to do the same thing, retreating to their own room up the hall and closing the door behind them.

Sam lay under the covers of her bed, still fully clothed, still wearing sneakers. She stared at the ceiling, listening to the sounds outside. She rarely heard crickets in LA, and they were practically an orchestra here, perpetually warming up their instruments in a cricket-y cacophony.

When she couldn't wait even another minute, she slid out of bed and out the door. The floor creaked as she tiptoed up the hall. The moon wasn't full—not yet!—but its light streamed in through the front windows all the same, casting the kitchen in an eerie blue glow.

Sam was a hunter with a single purpose. She headed straight for her prey on the kitchen table, to that morass of dark cords. The mouse really was hiding in the shadows! She plucked it from the tangle carefully and followed its tail to the back of the computer. With a wiggle and a tug, it was free.

The mouse sat in her palm like a dead thing.

No, like a thing that was never alive. There was a difference.

She tried not to think about tomorrow, when Aunt Vicky would sit down to use the computer. Would she even be able to work? Would she miss her deadline?

Sam tried to squash the feelings of guilt. She couldn't let herself worry about that. Armen would have a mouse. He was her partner. They'd find a way. Sam needed it more.

She shoved the mouse into her pocket and snuck outside, careful not to let the door slam behind her.

The crickets played louder out here, and there were more of them. What sounded like an orchestra before was now a wild horde of barbarians. Even the forest seemed changed. Shadows had swarmed over it, had eaten it up. There were no individual trees, not anymore—just a great maw of darkness waiting to swallow her up, too.

Voices wafted over from one of the windows. Aunt Vicky's voice. Sam took another look at the forest and crept along the house. She wasn't trying to listen.

You'd better not have been eavesdropping. I won't tell you again.

But she also couldn't help hearing, now that she was right here.

"...it's not." Aunt Vicky's voice was broken and stilted, as if she were crying. "Seeing them there, the looks on their faces... It all came back. All of it."

"It's okay," Hannah said, and then she asked a question that Sam couldn't hear.

"Saturday," Aunt Vicky said. "How am I going to get through tomorrow? What if they ask me about Grant?"

Grant was her father's name. Sam pressed her palm against the side of the house to keep her balance. They were talking about the caseworker coming tomorrow, and about Sam's dad. Aunt Vicky's brother. Why would the caseworker ask about him? Hadn't Sam answered enough questions about her father for a lifetime already? And besides, Aunt Vicky didn't even know him. She didn't know anything!

"I know it's not easy, Vic, but it's going to be okay. I swear, it will be," Hannah said. "Let me call your therapist now. I'll leave a message on her machine."

Aunt Vicky let out another sob. "What if I become just like him? Just like my mother? I didn't have kids for a reason, Hannah. You know that. You know why."

A ball of thorns formed in Sam's throat, making it hard to swallow.

"Come away from the window," a familiar voice said from behind Sam. "Nothing good will come from spying."

Sam turned and found Ashander leaning against a tree at the edge of the forest, barely visible in the shadows. She took a step toward him.

"There's a smart girl," he said with a grin. "Now let's see if you've passed the first test."

FROM THE RULES FOR FOX & SQUIRRELS

EARN THE FOX'S FAVOR

To earn the Fox's favor, you must offer him cards from your hand—even though you've been saving those cards for scoring. Even though those cards represent the nuts that will help you survive winter.

The Fox demands unwavering loyalty. Do whatever you must to prove it.

CHAPTER NINE

AS SAM WALKED toward Ashander, Aunt Vicky's voice faded away, replaced by a ghostly, rhythmic chorus of crickets. Soon she could hear nothing of the conversation behind her. In fact, she wouldn't have been surprised to turn around and find the house itself entirely gone, swallowed up by the night.

Ashander, his fur and hat and fancy coat turned gray and silver in the moonlight, beckoned her closer. The wind seemed to push Sam from behind, tousling her hair and urging her to obey.

"Well?" he asked. "Did you solve the riddle?"

"I think so," Sam said. She felt as if she were at the top of a roller coaster, in that weightless moment before the coaster plunged over the edge and the ride became either thrilling or terrifying. *Or both.* She swallowed. "The answer is . . . a mouse."

Ashander's eyes lit up like flames. "Very good, Samantha!"

Sam felt an echoing warmth inside her chest. Until this moment, she hadn't realized how badly she wanted to impress Ashander. To make him proud.

"And did you bring me my prize?" Ashander asked, leaning toward her. He licked his lips and rubbed his paws together, as if he was expecting a tasty treat.

Which he probably was.

Sam's sudden blaze of satisfaction died out immediately. She wrapped her hand around the computer mouse in her pocket. This was a mistake. A huge mistake. She didn't know how Ashander would react. Would he think she was trying to cheat? But it was too late to back out of her plan now. All she could do was forge onward and pretend she had all the confidence in the world. Be like Caitlin.

"Yes," Sam said, and her voice only wavered a little. "I caught one for you."

She held out the mouse on her palm. Its cord tail dangled almost all the way to the ground.

Ashander stared at it, his face unreadable.

The fox's whiskers bristled. Was he angry?

His ear twitched. Was he surprised?

Sam's heart gave a single rabbit hop. She took a small step back.

And then Ashander lifted his foxy chin and laughed. *Laughed!*

"Oh, you are a clever one, Sam," he said, wiping a tear from his eye.

Sam was so relieved that she wanted to laugh herself.

"And I especially appreciate that the prize you've brought me belongs to someone else. Your aunt, am I right? Excellent choice!" Ashander said as his chuckle faded. "There's no fun in stealing things that are already ours."

He took the mouse from Sam's hand. His fur tickled her palm, his claws lightly scratching her skin.

"Yes, yes. Quite clever," he said again, although this time he seemed to be talking to himself.

"So . . . did I pass the test?" Sam asked. She wanted to hear him say it. She wanted there to be no doubt.

He swung the mouse by its tail. In his hands, the simple piece of office equipment seemed to dance and spin as if it were alive.

"Oh, you passed, dear girl," Ashander said. "You have officially won my trust."

Sam shivered as if a spell had covered her in sparkles. She'd done it! She'd passed the first test! She was one step closer to the Golden Acorn, and to her parents, and to *home*. She was so excited that she almost didn't hear Ashander mutter softly, "I hope for your sake that you keep it."

"I will," Sam said solemnly, even though she wanted to do a victory dance around the whole forest. "I will be worthy of your trust!"

"That's what I like to hear," he continued. "Are you ready for the second test? Or perhaps you've had enough excitement for a while. You need a break! Perhaps some tea and scones and a good long sleep by the fire . . ."

"No!" She looked at her watch. Not at the time, but at the tiny glowing moon, almost full. "What do I have to do?"

Ashander continued spinning the computer mouse. "Well, I did have a test in mind—a good one, too. I was going to send you to the tallest tree in the forest to catch an owl. Oh, how much fun you would have had, up that high without a net! And owl claws are so notoriously *long* and *sharp* . . ."

Sam gulped. If that was the test he wasn't giving her, then she wasn't sure she wanted to know what was worse.

"But I'm starting to think that might be too easy for you. And we must work hard for the things we want." Ashander smiled. "Now that your aunt Vicky is part of this, I think she should stay a part of it, don't you?"

"What? No!" Sam said. She already felt terrible for taking her aunt's computer mouse. "She doesn't know anything about this."

"Nor should she find out," Ashander replied. "You see, the second test . . . is the test of loyalty."

Loyalty. Sam shivered again. Heroes were always loyal. They never told the enemy their plans, even when they were captured. Sam winced a little, remembering the night BriAnn had stayed over and Sam had made a bad joke about her father's temper. Her mother had driven BriAnn home immediately. *He's your father, Samantha. You owe him everything.*

Sam understood loyalty now. She wouldn't make that mistake again.

"Here, then, is your new test," Ashander said. "Pay it heed, for I will only say it once."

"I'm ready," Sam said, wishing she had one of those fancy phones that could record things.

Ashander took a step back, deeper into the shadows. Now the moonlight shone only on his muzzle, and his eyes were merely glints in the darkness. He spoke with a whispered voice that seemed to come from both him and the forest at the same time.

A gift more precious than it seems,
it is the very stuff of dreams.
Beloved! Behold
its radiant gold
brings joy to she who holds it dear.
Prove loyalty, and bring it here!

Sam repeated it in her head as fast as she could, over and over—*Beloved! Behold its radiant*—but Ashander didn't wait for her to finish as the squirrels had.

"You've a fast brain, Samantha," the fox said. "We shall see if you've the loyalty to match."

Brings joy to she who holds it dear—

"And since time is running out, you'll need a good deal of both."

Prove loyalty, and bring it here!

There, she had it memorized! She did!

"Why so quiet?" Ashander asked. "Fox got your tongue?"

"I'll figure it out. I promise," Sam said. She saw the computer mouse still in his hand and decided to take a risk. What was one more when she had already taken so many? "Since you can't eat the mouse I brought, I could . . . Could I take it back?" If she was careful, she could slip it right back into the mess of computer cords on the table and Aunt Vicky would never miss it.

Ashander stepped toward her, and the moon drenched him in eerie light. He held out the mouse in his open palm.

Sam hesitated. He seemed perfectly at ease and as dashing as ever. No hardness in his eyes. Those weren't always reliable signs, but sometimes they were.

She reached for the mouse. As her first fingertip brushed the smooth plastic, Ashander yanked it away.

"No," he said quietly. "You may *not* have it back. These are not friendly favors, girl; they are *tests*. You want the Golden Acorn, and this is the price."

An animal howled in the distance, as if in warning.

Sam flinched. "I . . . I understand."

Ashander stared at her and she saw it, the glimmer of something dangerous in his eyes. But then he smiled his old foxy smile and held his arms wide. "You're doing well, Sam. Very well, indeed! Keep it up, and you'll soon find yourself back where you want to be. Till tomorrow, then."

He bowed with a great flourish and stepped backward into the forest. The shadows engulfed him immediately.

Sam stood alone in the moonlight, her breath coming shallow and fast, and tried to still the shaking in her legs. The forest felt emptier without Ashander, as if by leaving he had also taken the very wind and leaves.

"Hail and well met, Sam!" a tiny voice called. Birch raced out from behind a tree, followed by Cedar. Behind them, walking on her hind legs in a far more stately fashion, was Maple. Sam was so relieved to see them that she almost clapped.

"Congratulations, Sam," Maple said. "We knew you would pass the first test!"

Cedar lifted an acorn cap holding three tiny confections. "We made you celebration tarts, but I ate mine on the way here. I could also eat yours, if you don't want it."

"Rude!" Birch chided. "At least let Sam admire my handiwork before it disappears. I mashed the acorn meat particularly well." She looked up at Sam with the white ruff of her chest puffed out. "Swordplay isn't the only thing I'm good at."

"I can see that!" Sam said, genuinely delighted. She was slightly less excited at the prospect of eating *acorn meat*.

Still, people didn't bake special treats for her that often. Her mom baked special cupcakes on report card day, and that one time Sam had gotten a truly awful haircut and cried for a whole afternoon, her mother had made a strawberry-rhubarb pie. But right now, it was Aunt Vicky's chocolate birthday cake that came to mind most vividly. Probably because she'd just eaten it.

Sam knelt and admired the tiny acorn tarts. "Thank you for such an amazing gift. Look how perfectly round they are! Is that a leaf design on top?"

"Yes!" Birch said, and held her chin so high she was in danger of falling over backward.

Cedar eyed Sam expectantly, his paw already wrapped around another tart.

Sam winked at him. "I'm pretty full right now," she said, patting her stomach as if such a wee morsel of food could make a difference. "Would you please eat mine for me?"

Birch and Cedar needed no further prodding. They each shoved a tart into their mouths and then began play-fighting over the last one. Sam laughed. It felt good to be nice to the squirrels.

Maple sighed with a smile and came to stand by Sam's bent knee. The scarf around her neck fluttered softly.

"You impressed Ashander a great deal," Maple said quietly. "I have rarely seen him so proud!"

Sam felt herself puffing up, just like Birch had.

Maple put a soft paw on Sam's leg. "But . . . you took a risk with your clever answer. Please don't try to trick him again. It may go very differently if you do."

Sam wanted to brush off Maple's warning, to continue basking in the glow of her victory, but she remembered the look in Ashander's eyes when he'd mentioned the Golden Acorn and its price. She hugged her arms.

"I'll be careful," she told Maple.

It's what heroes were supposed to say, even if they didn't believe it.

CHAPTER TEN

MR. SANCHEZ—THEIR NEW caseworker—was due to arrive at ten, and Sam intended to spend every minute beforehand locked securely in her room. Aunt Vicky was bound to discover her missing computer mouse. What if she asked Sam about it? What if she somehow knew? What if Sam had left fingerprints, and Aunt Vicky or Hannah owned one of those personal crime kits and dusted the scene and ran her prints through the computer and—

"Caitlin! Sam!" Hannah called from the kitchen. "Breakfast!"

Well, there was no escaping her fate now.

Caitlin's door opened. Sam waited a beat before opening her own and was surprised to run smack into her sister.

"You can go to breakfast without me, you know," Caitlin said quietly.

"I know," Sam answered, chagrined.

"I know you know." Caitlin sighed, but not in a mean way. It was like she was trying to say something but didn't know how.

"What are you going to say today?" Sam asked. "If Mr. Sanchez asks."

Caitlin shrugged. "Same things I said last time, I guess."

"I mean about this place," Sam said. "About . . . how you like it here."

Caitlin held Sam's gaze. "I'm going to tell him the truth. It's a pretty nice place, and it's great having a treadmill in my room. Don't you think it's okay?"

Sam's mind filled with all the things she missed. The movie nights. The afternoon donuts at the food cart on their block. Her after-school "study sessions" with BriAnn where they did nothing but look at animals on pet adoption websites and assign them superpowers and new names.

"But what about your softball team?" Sam asked. "All your friends are in another state."

Caitlin leaned against the wall. "Yeah, well, they're still my friends even if they're not in front of my face every day. And I'll make new ones here. So will you."

Back home, Caitlin was a total grouch half the time when Sam asked her a question. It was weird that she actually answered things here, and without giving Sam a hard time.

"Just give Mr. Sanchez a chance, okay?" Caitlin asked.

Grudgingly, Sam said, "Fine."

Caitlin punched Sam's shoulder playfully, like she some-times did to her softball friends. "There's the team spirit! Now let's go eat. I'm half dead from starving."

Aunt Vicky and Hannah bustled around the kitchen, pouring cereal, wiping surfaces, and trying to find cabinet space for all the mugs and dishes that seemed permanently at home on the countertops. Sam ate breakfast and tried not to stare at the computers on the table. More specifically, at what was missing from the computers.

As if she could read Sam's thoughts, Aunt Vicky said, "Should we move the computers? Does it look bad that they're on the table where we eat?"

Sam spooned a huge heap of cereal flakes into her mouth and crunched furiously.

Hannah gave Aunt Vicky's arm a squeeze. "This is how we live, and that's what we want him to see. It's fine."

When someone said things were "fine," they almost never were.

But Sam didn't want to think about Mr. Sanchez's impending visit, or about what was going to happen when Aunt Vicky realized her mouse was gone. Instead, she ate her cereal and thought about her new test.

The riddle said the "gift" was precious, and that it "brings joy to she who holds it dear." Clearly it was something Aunt Vicky cherished. Sam would have to watch her closely to see what she loved. It might look suspicious to write everything down in a notebook, so she'd have to keep track in her head.

Today Aunt Vicky was wearing long shorts and a pink short-sleeved button-down shirt. No earrings or necklace that

Sam could see. A watch with a thick green strap clung to her wrist, and a plain gold ring circled one of her fingers.

Nothing seemed particularly special. Sam's mental notebook remained blank.

Mr. Sanchez arrived fifteen minutes before ten, while Aunt Vicky was still mopping the kitchen floor. She put the mop and bucket in the corner, wiped her hands on her shorts, and let him in.

Mr. Sanchez was taller than Sam's dad, with arms and shoulders like tree trunks, and he wore the tiniest wire-rimmed glasses Sam had ever seen. They looked like doll glasses on his big, square face. How did they even stay on?

A woman who introduced herself as Sally Overton-Black had come with him. She was tall, too, but more like a sapling with thin arms and dangly earrings.

Mr. Sanchez and Sally Overton-Black smiled a lot. Not as much as Hannah did, but still more than people who were responsible for keeping Sam from her parents should. And they wanted to talk to Sam first. *Alone.* That was nothing to smile about.

Sam sat at Aunt Vicky's kitchen table, her feet wrapped around the legs of the wooden chair, her hands toying with the silver ring she'd put on that morning for strength. She knew better than to scowl, but she was thinking it. *Scowl, scowl, scowl.*

Mr. Sanchez and Sally Overton-Black leaned back in their

chairs on the other side of the table and smiled and sipped from mugs of tea, before Hannah and Aunt Vicky and Caitlin all went outside to see the chickens.

"This is an informal conversation, Samantha," Mr. Sanchez said. "We know you've been through a lot of big changes lately, and we just want to see how you're doing." Sally nodded. And smiled. Mr. Sanchez adjusted his tiny glasses. "We're counting on you to help us, Sam. All you have to do is tell us the truth. Can you do that?"

They always said it like that. *Truth.* As if it were both fragile and indestructible at the same time.

"Everything is *fine*," Sam said. She wanted to cross her arms, but she knew how that would look, like she was being stubborn. Maybe even a little belligerent.

Which she definitely was.

Mr. Sanchez and Sally waited.

Sam unclenched her hands and snaked one into her pocket, where she'd hidden a playing card. The Page of Walnuts. The squirrel had been drawn with a determined expression that reminded her of Birch when she was wielding her twig sword.

The waiting continued. Sam hated the silence. She hated not knowing what they were thinking. Not knowing what they were going to do. After Caitlin's accident—which was the word Sam's mother used, but maybe not the *right* word— people asked Sam a lot of questions about what had happened.

Sam had stayed quiet. Stayed *loyal*. Heroes never gave up their secrets under duress. Sam had sipped water out of a paper cup, then secretly ripped the cup to pieces under the table.

But in the end, she'd given in. She'd told them things. She'd *talked*. Mostly to ease the tension but also because, sometimes, it felt kind of *good*.

Sam didn't want to tell Mr. Sanchez or Sally Overton-Black anything at all, but if she *had* to, she could tell them that she liked the chickens and didn't mind eating eggs every day. That there were way too many bugs here. That she'd made several new friends, but they were the fuzzy, four-legged-animal kind, and they talked.

But maybe Mr. Sanchez would use something she said as an excuse to keep her parents away, like Mrs. Washington had done before.

Sam pressed her lips closed even tighter. She was not willing to take the risk.

Movement caught her eye outside the window, a splash of red-and-white fur in the trees. She bit her lip and stared into the shadows—even during bright sunlight, they were still there, places where the light didn't reach. Sam didn't know how, but she sensed Ashander was standing in one of them, hidden.

He was waiting to see what she would say. To see whether she'd stay loyal.

"Everything is fine," Sam said again, determined to sound more convincing.

"It's okay if you miss your parents, Sam," Mr. Sanchez said. "Do you miss them?"

The question was so direct that it caught Sam off guard. She looked down so they wouldn't see her surprise. Of course she missed her own parents! She missed her mom humming in the morning, when she was reading magazines at the kitchen table with her coffee but no one else had come out of their rooms yet. She missed her father pausing the nature documentaries on TV to explain something interesting about an animal, something that even the documentary people didn't know. She missed going to Caitlin's games as a family, on the days that Caitlin played well and won.

But also . . . there were things she *didn't* miss.

Like Caitlin's games where she made a mistake, or lost. Like being sick with worry when she got a bad grade at school, or got caught passing notes with BriAnn and had to take a letter home to be signed.

But she was absolutely *not* going to say any of those things.

"It's also okay if you like it here," Mr. Sanchez continued. Sally started to say something, but Mr. Sanchez put his hand on her wrist. Just a little, slight touch. Sally settled back into her chair. "Your aunt Vicky is very glad to have you here, Sam. She's very glad that you're safe. She might not have figured out how to tell you that yet. This is a lot of change for her, too. But everyone wants what's best for you."

We only want what's best for you. Another line that all grown-ups liked to say. Did any of them actually mean it?

Sam stayed loyal. She stayed silent.

"Have you made any new friends?" Mr. Sanchez asked.

That question, at least, seemed safe to answer—and she was eager to change the subject. She nodded.

"Lucas," she said. "His dad's name is Armen."

Sally scribbled in a notebook.

"Can you tell me anything about Lucas?" Mr. Sanchez asked. "What does he like to do?"

"He knits without knowing what he's making," Sam said, "which I still think is really strange."

Mr. Sanchez and Sally both chuckled. Mr. Sanchez said, "That does sound strange."

"But he's also nice," Sam added quickly. She thought about how he had run back to get a Band-Aid.

"That's good. Have you been spending a lot of time with Lucas?"

"No, not since . . ." Sam trailed off. She hadn't seen Lucas since she'd thrown his compass at him. The very compass he'd tried to give her as a present. "No, I've been busy."

Mr. Sanchez and Sally asked her a few more questions about Lucas and his father. She answered blandly, trying not to give them too much information.

Back in Los Angeles, people always wanted to know about her father, about what he'd done. They'd asked her general questions at first and then very specific ones about that last night. She was on guard for those kinds of questions from Mr.

Sanchez, but they never came. Before long, Mr. Sanchez nodded to Sally, and she closed her notebook.

He adjusted his glasses on his nose and peered closely at Sam. "Is there anything you'd like to tell us, or ask us?"

A million questions popped into her head: *Where are my parents now? Are they okay? Do they miss me? Are they coming to visit? When can we go home?* She knew she shouldn't ask any of them, but—

"When can I see my parents?" Sam blurted.

Mr. Sanchez did not look surprised by her outburst, but he did take a moment to think before answering. "Your parents have a list of things they need to do before they have permission to see you, Sam. Whether they do those things or not is up to them. Our priority is to keep you and your sister safe. But no matter what, it will take some time. Okay?"

Sam nodded, even though she felt entirely numb. Even though her heart felt like it was filled with stones.

It wasn't fair. None of this was fair.

"Do you have any other questions?" Sally asked.

"No," Sam said sharply.

Mr. Sanchez looked the tiniest bit sad. "Then thank you so much for your time, Samantha. Can you go outside and ask your sister to come in, please?"

Sam thought she'd misheard. Was she really done?

"It's not always going to be so hard, Sam," Mr. Sanchez said. "It'll get easier. You'll see."

Sam had no intention of being here long enough for it to get easier. In fact, this was probably the last time she would ever see Mr. Sanchez or Sally Overton-Black, and she was perfectly okay with that.

She stood up, her chair scraping loudly across the floor, and started to head outside. As she reached for the doorknob, she glanced out the window and saw Aunt Vicky talking with Armen and Hannah by the chicken coop.

Everyone was out of the house except Sam. *Everyone.* This was her one chance to sneak into Aunt Vicky's room unnoticed and figure out the answer to the second riddle.

If Sam could prove her loyalty to Ashander and get the Golden Acorn, then it wouldn't matter if her parents followed any of Mr. Sanchez's awful rules.

"Is it okay if I use the bathroom first?" Sam asked loudly.

Mr. Sanchez was busy scribbling notes on his pad. He hadn't touched it once while they'd been talking, but now, apparently, he had a lot to say.

"Of course you can," Sally said. She gave Sam a big smile, then started writing on her own pad in large, loopy script.

Good.

Sam headed down the hallway, but instead of going into the bathroom, she slipped inside her aunt's room.

Aunt Vicky and Hannah had the biggest bedroom in the house, but it was still smaller than Sam's room back home. One long dresser sat along the far wall, its surface covered in plants and stacks of folded clothes, with a big giraffe lamp standing guard from one end. The riddle had described the object she was supposed to steal as *radiant gold*. The giraffe was yellowish, so it went on Sam's mental list.

Over the dresser hung a mosaic of mirrors in all shapes and sizes, mixed in with framed photos. Sam perused them for clues, but they were mostly of smiling people who Sam didn't recognize.

A big queen bed sat in the middle of the room, under the window. Squat nightstands flanked it on both sides. One of the nightstands was covered in books, and if she'd had more time, Sam would have sat and read every last title. But none of them had gold covers or sparkled, and therefore none of them were the answer to the riddle.

Before she could assess the contents of the other nightstand, her eyes stopped on the pile of green and blue pillows at the head of the bed . . . and on the creature practically holding court from the middle of them.

A faded yellow rabbit sat atop the pillows, only this particular rabbit was holding a small stuffed scimitar and wearing an eyepatch . . . just like some of the animals in Aunt Vicky's bins.

Except this rabbit wasn't in a bin. It was clearly special. Maybe even *precious*, like in the riddle.

Sam tiptoed to the bed and stroked the bunny's ear. It was still soft, despite looking like it had waged and won a hundred battles.

Did it fit the other qualities mentioned in the riddle? Was it the *very stuff of dreams*? It was stuffed, certainly, so that part fit. Not even Ashander could argue with her logic! But the dreams part was confusing.

Sam added the bunny to her list of things Aunt Vicky might love and checked her watch. The moon glared at her from the watch face. Only the tiniest silver lining was still missing. She had so little time! And she'd already been in the room several minutes. Mr. Sanchez or Sally might be getting suspicious.

But before she opened the door, she went back to the pictures on the wall and looked at them more carefully. There were a dozen at least, and lots of them seemed to be photos of Aunt Vicky and Hannah with Hannah's family.

Nowhere, not in any picture, was Sam's dad.

It was like he'd been completely erased from Aunt Vicky's life.

Sam clenched her jaw. That's what they wanted Sam to do, too. To erase her own father and mother. To forget them completely. To betray them.

Never, Sam vowed silently. She could prove her loyalty to Ashander and her parents at the same time. Once she had the Golden Acorn, it was Oregon that she'd forget.

From the Rules for Fox & Squirrels

EARN THE FOX'S FAVOR (CONT'D)

A happy Fox requires very little effort to please. Give the Fox a pair of matching cards, and he'll stay happy. You can continue on with your day.

Earning the favor of a charming Fox is trickier. Sometimes three cards of the same number will appease him, and sometimes he wants three cards with their numbers all in a row. It's all about what the Fox wants in that particular moment, and no one knows what that is except the Fox!

Try everything you can think of.

Be as clever as you dare.

Hope for the best.

CHAPTER ELEVEN

NEITHER MR. SANCHEZ nor Sally Overton-Black questioned Sam as she left the house. She stepped outside and was welcomed by a wall of heat and sun. August in Oregon wasn't as hot as August in Los Angeles, but today it was trying. And it was a sticky warmth here, the kind that instantly coated her skin with sweat and made her shirt stick to her back.

Sam surveyed the yard. Aunt Vicky and Hannah stood by the chicken coop talking to Armen, while Lucas and Caitlin stood in the shade of a nearby tree. There was no sign of Ashander, but that didn't mean he was gone. He could still be out there, watching. It made Sam feel special to know that she mattered to him. And to know that even in a normal-looking yard, there was still magic at work.

But now she was supposed to send Caitlin inside, and that meant interacting with Lucas. Sam gnawed her lip. After their fight yesterday, that did not seem like an appealing prospect. She tried waving at Caitlin from a distance, but her sister didn't notice. With a sigh and a gut full of lead, she walked over.

Aunt Vicky and Hannah watched as Sam crossed the yard. They didn't just glance over and then turn back to their conversation—they watched the *whole time* and even smiled. It was . . . *odd*. Sam knew how to enter and leave a room in Caitlin's shadow, how to hide in her room when she heard loud voices, how to eat a meal without ever once looking up into anyone's eyes. But it was different here with Aunt Vicky and Hannah. They always found her. Sometimes it felt like having a spotlight pointed right at her face. She gave them a little nod, and it seemed to make them happy.

Lucas was in the middle of some story about a camping trip but fell silent as Sam approached. She was too embarrassed to look him in the eye and focused on her sister instead.

"How did it go?" Caitlin asked with her earbuds still in.

"Okay," Sam said, and shrugged. "They want to talk to you now."

Caitlin nodded, playing it cool. She turned and headed toward the house.

Sam wasn't fooled. She could see the hardness at the edge of her sister's mouth, and in her shoulders. The way she seemed to be putting on another piece of armor with every step.

Why hadn't Sam said something encouraging? *It wasn't so bad. They seem nice for people keeping our family apart.* Or even, *They didn't ask about that night.* Anything to make Caitlin less nervous. Caitlin would have done that for her.

"Hey," Lucas said, knitting furiously. Sam hadn't even noticed him take the needles from his bag.

113

"Um, hey," she said.

Sam watched him knit as the silence stretched between them, thin and brittle. It would take so little to shatter it, and yet Sam couldn't figure out how. Luckily, Aunt Vicky joined them, though it probably meant being subjected to even more questions.

"Are you okay?" her aunt asked.

Surprised, Sam nodded.

Not *What did you tell them? What did you say?* Only . . . *Are you okay?*

"Do you have any advice?" Aunt Vicky wiped her palms on her shorts. "I haven't done this before."

Sam thought about it; she really was an expert at this point. "They want you to be honest," she said finally. "They're really big on that."

"I can do that. Honesty is one of my best skills," Aunt Vicky said, and she looked up at the trees instead of at Sam. Sam looked away from people, too, sometimes. When she was nervous.

"They also want you to talk a lot." Then, to put Aunt Vicky more at ease, Sam added, "But I'm not great at that part."

Aunt Vicky nodded. "Me, neither. I always think of what I want to say afterward, but never right when I'm supposed to be saying it."

"Me, too!" Sam burst out, then shrank back again, suddenly overwhelmed with guilt. *It was a test of loyalty,* she reminded herself. It didn't matter if Aunt Vicky was nice to her. She had to stop wobbling and stay focused on the quest. She had to actually *be loyal.*

Which meant she should use this moment to find out more about her aunt. To maybe find out what she loved.

"Is that your wedding ring?" Sam pointed to her aunt's hand, ignoring the fresh pang of guilt as she did so.

Aunt Vicky held her hand out for Sam and Lucas. Sam peered closely, trying to hide her interest. The gold band was dinged and smudged, but it was kind of *radiant*, like in the riddle. Aunt Vicky said, "I wanted something simple. It has an inscription on the inside, the first thing Hannah said to me on the day we met. Hers has what I answered."

"What does it say?" Sam asked. She realized she wasn't asking just for the test, but because she actually wanted to know.

"Yeah, was it a knock-knock joke?" Lucas asked. "That would be funny."

Aunt Vicky laughed. "No. We were in college, and I was working on my laptop in a very busy coffee shop. Hannah asked if she could share my table. When I looked up and saw her, she was so pretty that I couldn't think. My brain just . . . went away. I said, 'Yes, I'd like another latte.'"

Sam laughed in spite of herself.

"I don't get it," Lucas said, but he was laughing, too.

"Neither did she," Aunt Vicky said. "Lucky for me, she found—finds—my social ineptitude charming."

Sam liked the story. She didn't want to, but she couldn't

help it. It made her think of her mother sitting at the kitchen table in their condo, drinking her glass of red wine and twisting her own wedding and engagement rings around her finger. Around and around, as if she were trying to secure them in place or take them off.

Aunt Vicky glanced over toward the chicken coop and Hannah. The lines around her eyes softened and faded, and a smile tugged at the corners of her mouth.

She seemed to really love her wife. The riddle contained the word *beloved*, which was often used in weddings. Maybe getting married was *the stuff of dreams* for Aunt Vicky. But how could Ashander expect her to take her aunt's wedding ring? What a horrible thing to do, especially now that Sam knew how much it meant to her . . . and probably to Hannah, too.

But that's what loyalty meant, right? Staying true to someone no matter what happened. No matter what awful thing they told you to do.

Sam needed to keep looking. Maybe there was something else that Aunt Vicky loved even more. *A gift more precious than it seems.*

When Aunt Vicky looked back at Sam, her gaze caught on Sam's hand. Sam realized she'd put on the ring with the blue stone—the ring from Aunt Vicky's plastic bin—for her talk with Mr. Sanchez and never taken it off. Her mouth felt dry, and she couldn't swallow. She covered the ring with her other hand, but she knew she was too late.

"Lucas, go talk to your father for a minute," Aunt Vicky said. "I'd like to talk to Sam alone."

"Sure!" Lucas said, stowing his knitting.

"He doesn't have to go—" Sam said, frantic. Suddenly she wanted him here, wanted him close. Where was Caitlin?

Lucas gave Sam a puzzled look.

"It's okay," Aunt Vicky said calmly. She nodded to Lucas, and he headed off. "I'm not angry, Sam. I just wanted to talk to you alone. But we're not really alone, see? Hannah and Armen are right there, and Sally and David—Mr. Sanchez— are just through that door with your sister. So you're safe, okay?"

Sam's heart beat so fast that answering was not an option. She managed to nod. Not because she believed her aunt, but because she knew she was supposed to.

Aunt Vicky put her back against the tree trunk, not so much leaning as collapsing. "I used to collect stuffed animals," she said slowly. "They covered my bed and filled up every corner of my room. My mother used to say I had too many, and that I was going to drown in them. But every single one of them had a name and a personality."

Sam said nothing. She could not move. She didn't expect Ashander to come to her rescue, but silently she begged Maple to appear, or Birch, or even Cedar.

"But you already knew about the stuffed animals, didn't you?" Aunt Vicky asked. She pointed to the ring on Sam's hand.

"I'm sorry. I—" Sam said. "I'll give it back."

"That ring used to be the crown for the Queen of Squirrels," Aunt Vicky continued. "I could never get it to stay on her head, so she wore it on her tail."

That's where Sam had found it, on the stuffed squirrel's tail. The stone was the same blue as Maple's dress.

Sam twisted the ring off and held it in her shaking palm. "A crown?"

Aunt Vicky looked at the single cloud visible in the sky and seemed to choose each of her words carefully. "I had elaborate scenarios worked out. The queen's greatest ally was the Pirate Princess of Bundom. She was the good kind of pirate. The princess and I escaped to the high seas as often as possible." Aunt Vicky glanced at the ring in Sam's hand, but she didn't take it. "Those were very hard years in my life, Sam. But when I was struggling the most, Pirate Princess saved me. She was my best friend. She was always there for me, like your books are for you."

Sam looked away from her aunt's sad eyes, a thickness growing in her throat. *The quest*, she reminded herself, and swallowed down her guilt.

The Pirate Princess of Bundom sounded very much like the stuffed bunny Sam had seen on her aunt's bed. And the adventures Aunt Vicky was describing were most definitely the *stuff of dreams*.

And what could be more *precious* or *beloved*, what could

bring more *joy* or be held more *dear*, than the companion who helped get you through the bad times? Sam knew how she felt about her books, her stories.

Maybe the answer to the riddle wasn't the wedding ring at all.

"Do you still go on adventures?" Sam asked quietly, because how could she take the rabbit if Pirate Princess was still going on missions?

Aunt Vicky offered her a small smile. "No, we're both retired from the adventure business. I've got other ways to get through tough times now. A therapist. A wife. Some really good friends."

Sam held out the Queen of Squirrels' ring again. "I'm really sorry."

"No, you hold on to that for the queen and me," Aunt Vicky said. "There are a lot of dangers in these woods, Sam. You might need the queen's magic." She put her hand on Sam's shoulder, gently, and Sam got the impression that "the woods" didn't just mean the nearby trees.

"But there's no danger from me, Sam," her aunt continued. "There never will be."

Aunt Vicky clearly meant well, and Sam gave her a small nod to indicate that she'd heard. But promises were the wrapping paper around a gift, bright and appealing. You never knew what was actually inside until you opened the box.

Sam did slip the ring back on her finger, though, and it tingled against her skin.

Aunt Vicky wiped her eyes with the back of her wrist. "You

know what?" she asked, suddenly standing straighter. "I think now is the perfect time to learn how to hold a chicken. Don't you think? You're going to love it, Sam, I promise!" And just like that, she started walking toward the coop.

Sam's heart gave a little leap. A little *wobble*. This time, Sam let it.

Holding chickens!

Caitlin came out of the house and called for Hannah to go in next. Aunt Vicky motioned for her, too. "Come on, girls!"

Sam practically ran over to join them. She thought maybe Lucas would join, too, but he and his dad were leaning against the chicken fence, side by side, reading books. If there wasn't chicken-holding on the line, Sam could see herself joining them.

"You're going first," Aunt Vicky said to Caitlin.

Caitlin raised her cast. "Uh, did you forget about this?"

"I did not," Aunt Vicky said with a grin. "You only need one hand to hold a chicken properly." She bent and picked up a chicken with what seemed like no effort at all. And the chicken didn't even seem to mind! "You need to be firm," she said. "A chicken likes to know she's secure. That you've got her. The second she doubts you, that's when she makes a fuss and tries to get away."

Caitlin barely waited for Aunt Vicky to finish talking before she swooped down for her own chicken. It squawked and flapped its wings in her face.

"Adjust your grip like this," Aunt Vicky said, illustrating on her own chicken.

Caitlin's chicken calmed down almost instantly.

"Woo!" Caitlin said. "I'm holding a chicken! Sam, you've got to try this."

Aunt Vicky chuckled. "How about it, Sam? You ready to try?"

Sam nodded and pointed. There was one chicken she wanted to hold more than all the others.

"Oh, you've taken a shine to Lady Louise!" Aunt Vicky picked her up as if she was fielding a grounder at one of Caitlin's softball games. "Did you see what I showed your sister? Put your hand in this position, so her legs will be between your fingers."

Sam did as she was told, and a second later, Aunt Vicky plopped Lady Louise into her arms. A large feathered wing whacked her in the nose, so she gripped a little more firmly. "I've got you," she told the bird.

Lady Louise looked miffed, but settled. With the special grip, the chicken's head was practically nestled against Sam's chest, close to her underarm. She had her whole left hand free to pet Louise's soft feathers.

"Well done, Sam! She clearly respects you," Aunt Vicky said. "We're not convinced she actually *likes* anyone, so respect is the most you can hope for."

Sam stared into Lady Louise's pitch-black pebble eyes and grinned. She couldn't help it. There was a bird in her arms. And because of all the documentaries she'd watched with her dad, she knew that birds were actually dinosaurs, so . . .

There was a dinosaur in her arms!

Caitlin put her bird back on the ground, although it seemed more like the bird's idea than Caitlin's. "You're better at this than I am," she told Sam. "I'm going to call you Chicken Whisperer from now on."

As far as nicknames from Caitlin went, this was the best one ever.

"What does that make you, then?" Sam asked, feeling emboldened.

"I'm a chicken *wrangler*," Caitlin said. She had her earbuds in her hands, but still hadn't popped them in. "Just not a *good* chicken wrangler."

"Only way to get better is to try again," Aunt Vicky said, and just like that, she'd picked up another chicken and handed it to Caitlin. Caitlin was forced to shove her earbuds back in her pocket. That alone was a miracle.

Mr. Sanchez and Sally Overton-Black stayed for almost another full hour. They interviewed Aunt Vicky last, then toured the house and yard, and even drank iced tea as they met the chickens.

When the caseworkers had spoken with Sam and Caitlin back in LA, everyone had worn tight expressions on their faces the whole time. Even their first caseworker, Mrs. Washington. Every conversation had been full of sharp angles and pitfalls and booby traps, or else the opposite: too-soft voices dripping the same phrases over and over. *It's going to be all right. It will get better. We just want what's best . . .*

Now Sam went from laughing one moment to feeling guilty the next to joking with Aunt Vicky the moment after. It was starting to get exhausting. There were times when she had no idea which way to feel at all.

When Mr. Sanchez and Sally finally left, Mr. Sanchez waved from the passenger seat of their car and called, "Nice meeting you, Caitlin and Sam. See you again soon!"

He said it like he was their friend. Sam stood in the shade of the front porch with her hands shoved into her pockets. But Aunt Vicky and Hannah and Caitlin stood in the driveway and waved back.

"Drive safe," Hannah called.

Sam dodged aside as Aunt Vicky and Hannah went back inside, but stepped in front of her sister, blocking her way.

"Why did you wave to him?" Sam asked, genuinely confused. "He's trying to make us forget that we want to go home!"

The Caitlin that Sam knew would tell her to shut up. To go to her room. To stay quiet and out of the way.

This Caitlin shrugged. "Actually, I thought they were both pretty okay. Mr. Sanchez's glasses were a total dork-fest, though. I told him to up his game. We'll see if he does for next time."

She nudged Sam playfully with her shoulder. "Now move, nerd, I need more lemonade."

Sam stood on the porch, stunned, as Caitlin walked past her and into the house. Armen said something and Caitlin laughed. Not even with the fake laugh!

Caitlin kept looking forward to the future, as if that was going to save them. But Sam knew better. She knew what they'd had before. She and Caitlin had had a system, and it had worked just fine. All Sam needed to do was find a way back to it.

Caitlin used to be Sam's protector, but everything was different in Oregon, even that. Now it was Sam's turn to save them. She needed to steal Pirate Princess and win the Golden Acorn, and she needed to do it fast, before the Caitlin she knew slipped away completely.

CHAPTER TWELVE

DURING THE MORNING'S visit, Sam had almost forgotten about the stolen computer mouse. Now that it was lunchtime, she could think of nothing else.

"I can't find it anywhere," Aunt Vicky said, sorting through the computer cords for the third time. She turned to Armen. "Are you sure you didn't put it in your bag by mistake?"

Sam sat at the other end of the table with Caitlin and Lucas, trying to eat her egg-salad sandwich without choking on guilt. She'd been chewing the same bite for over a minute.

"I don't have it, Vic," Armen said. "I've searched my bag, but you can go through it yourself if that'll make you feel better."

Aunt Vicky took his bag and did just that.

Armen glanced at Sam's end of the table. "I don't suppose one of you children saw what happened to the mouse?"

Caitlin was about to answer when Aunt Vicky snapped, "Don't involve them! They don't even have computers."

Sam tried to swallow the gooey lump of food in her mouth but couldn't.

I had to do it, she said silently. *I'm sorry, but I had to.*

"I've got two extra mice at my house," Armen said. "I'll run back and get one."

Aunt Vicky blew the hair out of her eyes and attacked the computer cords again. "We're already so far behind."

The explosion was coming. Lucas continued eating like nothing was wrong, but Caitlin was stiff as a rock at Sam's side, bracing for the inevitable. She gave Sam a small, grim nod, letting her know that at least they were in it together. At this stage, there was nothing else they could do.

Hands. Hands were so fast.

Aunt Vicky stopped. Closed her eyes. Took a deep breath. Sam watched the hard line of her shoulders round and soften, as if Aunt Vicky were remolding them out of clay. She opened her eyes again.

"I'm sorry, Armen," Aunt Vicky said. "I was upset, and I shouldn't have snapped at you." She looked at Caitlin and Sam. "I'm sorry, kids."

"It's okay, no big deal," Caitlin said brightly, and went back to her sandwich.

Sam sat there silently, waiting for the surprise. The twist. The sharp knuckle of a fist that would jab an arm or a leg. Aunt Vicky had been so angry, Sam was sure of it. But now, she almost seemed back to normal.

Sam had never seen her father do anything like that. Not even once. And now everyone was acting like nothing had happened.

But then ... maybe nothing *had* happened. It was so confusing!

Aunt Vicky poured herself some iced tea and refilled Armen's glass. Sam studied the lines around her eyes, the set of her mouth, the position of her hands. The anger was gone. Somehow Aunt Vicky had banished it completely.

"Maybe Sam and Lucas can fetch the mouse," Aunt Vicky said. "That way, we can get started on the documentation."

"Oh, hooray, my favorite part," Armen said. "Lucas? Sam? Do you accept this highly important mission?"

"Sure!" Lucas said.

Sam nodded. She found herself pleased that Lucas was willing to spend time with her again after the whole compass-throwing incident.

"No dawdling," Armen said.

"A little dawdling is fine," Aunt Vicky countered. She smiled at Sam.

Caitlin polished off the last of her sandwich and rolled her eyes. "Is everyone in this house a complete nerd?"

Sam looked at Aunt Vicky, to see if she'd be upset. But her aunt only laughed.

"Oh, absolutely," Aunt Vicky said.

Sam finished her lunch and headed into the sunny

wilderness with Lucas. He had grabbed three Oreos on the way out and was shedding crumbs with every step. They walked along the edge of the forest, close enough to enjoy some shade but not so close that they'd be tripping on roots every three seconds.

For once, Lucas wasn't saying anything. Sam knew why. He was upset with her about the compass. It shouldn't have bothered her—she was leaving soon anyway!—but for some reason, it still did.

"Um . . . I'm sorry for yesterday," Sam said.

Lucas's eyes widened. "What? I told my dad what happened, and he said I was a huge jerk to you."

"He called you a jerk?"

"Well, not exactly," Lucas said. "He said that if you don't want to talk about . . ." He paused. "He said that if you don't want to talk about something, it's not my place to keep talking about it anyway. He said I was inconsiderate of your feelings, or something like that."

Sam walked in silence, thinking. Was that what had happened? Maybe it was. Maybe what happened wasn't entirely her fault.

"But I shouldn't have thrown the compass at you," she said.

"Yeah, my dad agrees about that, but he said your anger was understandable on account of my jerkishness."

Sam doubted those were Armen's exact words, but she got the gist.

"It's a good thing you missed," Lucas said.

"I didn't miss! I was aiming for your feet!"

Lucas laughed and, after a few seconds, so did Sam.

She took a chance. "I . . . don't suppose I could have the compass back?" She'd be looking for the Golden Acorn soon, and it might come in handy. Not that she could tell Lucas that.

He dug into his satchel and pulled it out. "I kept it just in case."

Sam gratefully took the compass and waited for the caveats. *Only if you promise not to throw it again. Only if you get good grades. Only if you do all your chores.*

Instead, Lucas pointed at a mushroom clinging to a nearby tree and proceeded to tell her everything he knew about it. Probably everything *anybody* knew about it, considering how long he talked. Surprisingly, Sam didn't mind. She opened her compass and watched the needle find its way north.

When they got to Armen and Lucas's house—which looked a lot like Aunt Vicky's, only it was gray with white trim and there were no chickens—Sam drank a glass of water in the small, tidy kitchen while Lucas searched his father's desk for the extra computer mouse. Among the items Lucas tossed to the floor during his excavation was a box of white envelopes.

"Oh!" Sam said. "Do you think I could borrow one of those envelopes? I have to send a letter to my best friend."

She felt another pang of guilt. What with Mr. Sanchez's visit and the chickens and everything, she'd barely thought about BriAnn all day.

"Sure," Lucas said, handing her four of them. "The extras are for mistakes." A moment later, he yanked a white computer mouse out of the bottom drawer and held it up like a trophy. "Ta-da!"

Sam wasn't surprised to sense Ashander in the forest as they walked back to Aunt Vicky's. The sunlight played tricks, casting leaves with tints of red like his fur, turning shadows from black to purple, like his coat. Or maybe it wasn't the sun playing tricks, but the fox himself.

Either way, Sam got the message: Lucas was a distraction.

She wasn't his friend, and she didn't *want* to be his friend . . . not when BriAnn and her parents were waiting for her. This was just another part of her loyalty test.

"You got quiet," Lucas said.

"I guess I don't feel like talking anymore," Sam said.

He pulled out his knitting, and Sam tried not to look as terrible as she felt.

After dinner—it was quiche this time, which was still eggs but fancier—Armen and Lucas went home. Sam was wiping down the table and waiting for Caitlin to leap up and offer to help with the dishes, like she'd done after every meal. Instead, her sister dumped her plate on the counter and started to head back to her room.

Maybe she'd just forgotten.

Hannah seemed equally baffled. "Can you please stay and help with the dishes, Caitlin?"

Sam was positive Caitlin would now fall over herself for the chance to please every adult within range.

Caitlin paused in the hallway, a strange look of disinterest on her face. "I don't really feel like it tonight."

Sam's mouth fell open. Literally. Fell. Open.

Hannah recovered much faster. "When someone else cooks, the rest of us clean. It's a house rule."

"It'll only take you a few minutes," Aunt Vicky said, clearly trying to smooth things over. She'd cooked the quiche, but she was already putting foil on the leftovers. "We'd appreciate your help."

Caitlin sighed heavily, as if they'd just asked her to clean the Augean stables, like one of Hercules's labors. Finally, she said, "Whatever" and stomped back toward the kitchen.

Sam couldn't take her eyes off Caitlin. Who was this person? What had happened to her sister?

She knew Caitlin was changing, but she hadn't realized how fast.

Sam needed Pirate Princess, and she needed her *now*. Maybe she could sneak out while everyone was cleaning.

She cleared her throat. "I finished with the table. Is it okay if I go outside? I want to draw the chickens for BriAnn."

Aunt Vicky grinned so big. "Sure, go ahead! They've already been fed, so they should be in the coop, a bunch of contented little lumps."

"Thanks," Sam said, and scurried back to her room. It took her all of one minute to dump out her backpack, check the hallway, and then sneak into Aunt Vicky's room.

Pirate Princess was waiting for her, scimitar out, eyepatch in place.

"I'm sorry," Sam whispered, and she was. She took the stuffed animal from the bed and gently placed her in the backpack, careful not to catch her bunny ears in the zipper.

There was no going back after this. It wasn't like with the computer mouse. There was no spare Pirate Princess and no one else who could have taken her.

Aunt Vicky would know.

Aunt Vicky would never forgive her.

Sam hesitated. What was she doing?

What she had to do.

A show of loyalty.

For Ashander, and also for herself.

Sam glanced at the photographs on the wall. She shouldn't have forgotten BriAnn today, and she would never forget her parents. This place would not change her like it was changing Caitlin.

Her hand shook as she reached for the bedroom doorknob, but she still managed to turn it. Her legs wobbled as they carried her up the hall and through the kitchen, but she still managed to reach the door.

"Don't stay out after dark," Hannah called.

"I won't," Sam said, and pushed outside.

CHAPTER THIRTEEN

THE AIR WAS still warm and soupy-thick, even at almost eight. Long shadows stretched across the chicken yard like inky fingers, and they seemed to be growing longer by the minute. The sun set so late this far north!

Sam put BriAnn's newly addressed envelope in the mailbox and lifted the flag. The chicken yard was empty, just as Aunt Vicky predicted, the hens all cozy inside the coop. Sam wanted to join them. Maybe even to try to draw one, like she'd said.

"*Psst!*" a small voice called. "Sam!"

It took her a moment to find Birch at the edge of the forest, waving her twig sword. Maple stood next to her, tapping her tiny foot. "He's waiting, Sam!"

Sam sighed. So much for the chickens. She checked the house to make sure no one was watching, then hurried to join the squirrels in the forest.

The air cooled immediately, and the breeze grew bolder.

The fading sun speckled the ground with light, but the trees didn't allow any big spots to sneak through their branchy fingers. A bird's clear voice echoed but it was quickly drowned out by raspy, croaking toads and a hum of crickets.

"We weren't sure you were coming," Birch said, falling into step beside Sam.

"I was certain that you were," Maple said, her little chin raised. "I have great faith in you, Sam."

Sam puffed from the praise. The night seemed a little more welcoming all of a sudden. "Where's Cedar?" she asked.

"With Ashander," Birch replied, her mouth in a grim line. "Cedar made a joke that Ashander didn't like and—"

"*Shh*, now," Maple said. "That's enough of that."

Birch fell silent immediately, but she gave Sam a look that said, "You know what I mean."

And Sam did.

"Ashander is in no mood for games tonight, Sam," Maple said, her voice worried. And maybe a little tired. Her blue scarf fluttered around her neck in the breeze. "Have you brought him what he wanted?"

Sam swung her backpack around so she could hug it close. So she could hug Pirate Princess. "Yes, I think so."

Birch sighed. "It's not like you can ever be sure anyway."

Maple shushed them both this time. "Quiet now. Everything will be fine." Then she muttered, "Yes, yes. Absolutely fine."

The skies darkened, and the shadows joined together into even bigger pools of darkness. A scraggly bush scraped Sam's shin as they walked. A pebble wiggled its way into her sock.

Sam ducked under a hanging branch, and suddenly Ashander was there, sitting with his back against a tree just a few feet in front of her. The remaining rays of sunlight hit him at a steep angle, elongating his foxy snout and fangs. He picked at his teeth with one long claw.

Cedar had been juggling at Ashander's feet but dropped his pebbles when he saw Sam.

"Finally," Ashander said lazily.

"I brought the prize," Sam said. She felt a little stronger with Maple and Birch at her side, but her voice still came out shallow.

"Did you, now?" Ashander asked. He rolled his head to the side, and the darkening shadows danced over his fur. "I hope you didn't try to be too clever this time."

"The riddle could have several answers," Sam said. She cleared her throat. "I brought the only prize good enough for you."

"Oh, this should be fun," Ashander said. He leaned toward her. "Do tell, Samantha."

"The answer to the first riddle was a mouse, which is one of the favorite prey of the fox," she said, sounding like one of her dad's nature documentaries. "It seemed only right to bring you another of your favorite creatures for this test."

Sam turned away from Ashander, unzipped the backpack,

and carefully pulled Pirate Princess from its confines. The rabbit's scimitar had gotten bent, so Sam straightened it. And adjusted her eyepatch, too, for good measure. She knew Pirate Princess would want to look her best.

It was hard not to kiss the rabbit on top of her soft head, to whisper again how sorry she was, but Sam managed. She turned back to Ashander and held Pirate Princess aloft for everyone to see.

Ashander was on his feet like the snap of a whip. Sam forced herself to stand still, to hold her ground, even though he seemed so big tonight, so much taller than a normal fox. Even taller than she was. But she knew better than to flinch.

The fox stalked closer. Sam wanted to look at the squirrels, to see if they were safe, to see if they were still by her side, but she knew it was wiser to watch him. *Only* him.

Ashander took the rabbit's chin in his red paw. There was a gleam in his eye that Sam hadn't seen before.

"A rabbit," he said, and broke into a grin. "But no *ordinary* rabbit. A creature greatly beloved. This is a foe I know well, though I have not seen her for many years." He tugged at the rabbit, but Sam wasn't quite ready to let go.

"Second thoughts?" Ashander asked. "You have not proven your loyalty until you actually complete the test."

Pirate Princess seemed so incredibly small and helpless in Sam's hand. Despite her sword. Despite her battle scars. But Sam couldn't give up now, and she doubted very much that Ashander would let her if she wanted to. Sam found Maple

standing just beyond Ashander's reach, and the squirrel gave Sam an urgent nod.

Sam released her hand and let Ashander take his prize.

"There, there," Ashander said, pulling the rabbit from her arms. "That wasn't so hard. And now you've proven your loyalty. Do you feel it?"

She felt *something*, although it was closer to a stomachache. She stared at Pirate Princess, already wishing she could take her back, carry her out of the forest, and hide her in the safety of Aunt Vicky's room.

It was too late for that now. Much too late.

"Yes, I feel it," Sam said, because she knew that's what Ashander wanted to hear.

"Good," he said. "Because the next test is the most important of all." He leaned toward Sam—so close she could count the whiskers on his face, could feel the warmth of his breath on her cheek. "And just so our clever girl doesn't decide to be too clever, I will tell you exactly what I want for the last test. You won't even have to guess . . ." He wrapped a tendril of her hair around his claw. "You won't have any way to twist out of doing what I ask."

Sam forced herself to stand still and hold his gaze.

"The final test is easy," Ashander said, and his dark eyes seemed to laugh. "Bring me what I want, and I will lead you to the Golden Acorn. You're almost there, Sam. The ultimate prize is within your grasp!"

He paused dramatically, and Sam felt the magic in the air, as if the whole forest was holding its breath with her.

Ashander continued, his voice like honey dripped over thorns. "To prove yourself to me once and for all, you must make a gift of *sacrifice*. No tricks, no twists, no cleverness. You must bring me the chicken known as Lady Louise."

No, Sam thought. And then she couldn't help it. "No, not her! Not Lady Louise. Please!" She looked for Maple and the squirrels, but they had disappeared. Hopefully they were hiding.

"I thought you missed your parents, Sam," Ashander said. "I thought you wanted everything to go back to the way it was. Are you too selfish to help your own family?" Ashander stroked Pirate Princess as he spoke, but the motion was anything but sweet.

"No, I'm not selfish," Sam said. "I'll bring you something else. Anything else!"

"I told you what I want," the fox said quietly. "Bring me Lady Louise, or I'll take something else from you instead. I'll take *everything*. And then you will never, ever get home."

Ashander lifted Pirate Princess above his head.

No, Sam thought again, but this time she didn't dare say it out loud.

Slowly, as if he were enjoying every second, Ashander ripped Pirate Princess's head from her body. It felt as if he were ripping Sam's heart in two at the same time. He tore into her stuffing and tossed it in the air like confetti. Sam shuddered. One of the bright white tufts clung to her arm, and she shook it off as if it were poisoned.

Pirate Princess was gone.

From the Rules for Fox & Squirrels

EARN THE FOX'S FAVOR (CONT'D)

If you draw a hunting Fox from the Harvest deck, then good luck, brave squirrel!

Try giving him four cards of the same kind. That may be enough to appease the savage beast.

But not always.

Sometimes you must sacrifice oh so much more.

Chapter Fourteen

SAM MADE IT back to the yard before full dark but could not bring herself to go inside the house. Pirate Princess was gone forever, and with her, any hope Sam had of somehow rescuing the princess and returning her to Aunt Vicky. Her hands would not stop shaking.

Sam pushed her fingers through the mesh of the chicken fence and tried to calm her breathing. Almost as if she knew Sam was there, Lady Louise appeared on the tiny ramp leading out of the coop. The chicken looked smaller now. More fragile. As if Ashander's demand had reminded even Lady Louise that, to a fox, she was still only prey.

Rip. Slash. Stuffing falling like snow to the forest floor.

Ashander said Sam only had one test left. That she was close to winning his favor and the Golden Acorn and her way home.

All the things Sam wanted.

Only . . . it was getting harder to focus on *why* she wanted them. Now, mixed in with her memories of Saturday morning brunches and late-night movies were memories of hiding under the covers while she waited for the yelling to stop. Of trying to cry softly in the bathroom because she knew it would be so much worse if anyone heard. Of standing outside the front door of their house after school, not wanting to go inside. Of sometimes wondering what it would be like to run away.

The door to Aunt Vicky's house opened, pulling Sam back to the present. Hannah called, "Sam, it's getting late!"

Sam's legs carried her inside. Her mouth smiled. Her hands took the last piece of cake and, somehow, got a bite of it to her mouth. Aunt Vicky handed her milk in a white mug with a bright-yellow chicken painted on the side that read, CLUCK TWICE FOR TEA.

Aunt Vicky was being too nice. *So nice that it hurt.*

"I'm tired," Sam blurted. She handed the mug back to Aunt Vicky without taking a single sip. "I need to go to bed."

She didn't deserve cake. Or milk. Not after what she'd done to Pirate Princess.

And to Aunt Vicky.

"Are you feeling all right?" Hannah asked. She was at Sam's side in an instant, the back of her hand pressed gently to Sam's forehead. "Sweaty but not feverish. Good. Same as it is for most of us at this time of year."

"She's fine," Caitlin said from the table. She had one earbud in and one out, and was eating the last few crumbs of her cake, one by one. Normally Caitlin saying anything was enough to shift focus away from Sam. Between the two of them, Caitlin was the Lady Louise. The one with her chin up and her chest out. The bigger one. The brave one.

But here in Oregon, where nothing worked like it was supposed to, Hannah didn't leave Sam's side. Aunt Vicky switched the mug of milk for a glass of water and pressed it into Sam's hand.

Sam drank. The cool rush down her throat cleared her head. For a moment, she felt a little better. A little stronger.

"Caitlin's right," Sam said. "I'm fine. I think I just want to go to bed early."

"Sure thing, sweetie," Hannah said.

"Tomorrow we'll get all those boxes out of your room," Aunt Vicky said. "We'll make it more *yours*."

The offer made Sam's insides ache. But Aunt Vicky wanted Sam to be excited, so Sam managed a small smile and thanked them for the cake, and was finally allowed to escape.

When she slipped into her room, the squirrels were waiting for her.

Maple stood on the windowsill, looking out into the night. Birch and Cedar tussled on the bed, rolling around each other so fast that Sam could barely tell which squirrel was which.

She shut the door quickly and tossed her backpack onto the floor.

"I'm so glad you're okay!" She wanted to pull all three of them into a big hug, but Maple's serious expression dissuaded her.

"Ashander sent us," Maple said. She rubbed her tiny arm. "He thought you looked upset during the test."

Sam had been upset. Because *Ashander* had upset her.

Birch and Cedar stopped playing. Birch's helmet had fallen off, and Cedar's yellow tunic was twisted almost backward. They stared up at her, waiting.

Could she trust them?

Would they turn around and tell Ashander everything she said?

She honestly didn't know.

"Now, now," Maple said. "Put your pajamas on. Climb into bed. You've had a long day. Birch, Cedar, fix that pillow you rumpled! Smooth those sheets!"

The squirrels scampered over her bed, tugging the blankets and making it look ever so much more appealing. Suddenly, every muscle in Sam's body seemed to ache, as if she'd been clenching them for hours. She changed her clothes and crawled under her blanket, as instructed. All three squirrels sat on the windowsill, their furry feet dangling over the edge.

"I miss BriAnn," Sam said. She hadn't meant to say it. It just slipped out, a little like tears.

"I know, dear," Maple said. "You'll see her again soon."

"She'll show you all the pictures she's drawn," Cedar added.

Birch crossed her arms and huffed. "And she'll probably ask you about *Hawaii*."

"Shh, now," Maple scolded. "Sam is only doing what's necessary to protect her family and her secrets. She knows the rules."

She did know the rules. *Never tell. Not even your best friend. Not even when your sister ends up in the hospital.*

"He didn't mean to scare you, Sam." Maple's voice was soft and gentle, and Sam found herself drifting to sleep.

She woke to the sound of clattering plates in the kitchen and birds singing outside the window. A sweet, piney breeze drifted over her, as if it were sweeping away the night. Plus, three tiny acorn-meat tarts sat on her pillow, and only two of them looked half-eaten.

It was a nice way to wake up, and Sam wondered if it would be terrible to just stay in bed a little longer, and maybe stay in Oregon a little longer, too. Mr. Sanchez said it would get easier.

Maybe . . . maybe he was right.

But then Ashander's threat came back to her. She could almost hear his voice in her ear. *Bring me Lady Louise, or I'll take something else from you instead.*

There was no stopping this quest now. Maple had warned her at the beginning about this one unbreakable rule. Sam only wished she could go back and heed the warning.

And now the moon was full, its glowing face filling the tiny cutout on her watch. Time was up.

She heard noises from the next room, and a second later, Caitlin popped open Sam's door.

"You slept through breakfast, nerd. Hannah already left for work."

"Learn to knock," Sam grumbled.

Caitlin ignored her. "Hey, I think Mom packed my suitcase, and she put this old team hoodie in. It's way too small for me, even without the cast. You want it?" She held up a faded blue hoodie with white writing: THE SHERMAN OAKS SHOOTING STARS.

"Um," Sam said.

"Sweet!" Caitlin tossed the hoodie onto Sam's face. The world went dark again under the thick cotton. "Now get out of bed. I think Aunt Vicky wants to talk to you about something."

Those words pinned Sam in place. *Aunt Vicky wants to talk to you.*

Caitlin left and Sam stayed under the sweatshirt, trying not to panic. She breathed in the familiar scent of lavender laundry detergent. The kind her mom used. Every piece of clothing Sam owned smelled like that lavender. But not if she failed today. If she didn't pass the final test, if she didn't win the Golden Acorn, then slowly but surely, that lavender would disappear, replaced by whatever detergent Aunt Vicky or Hannah bought.

That's what would happen to *everything* if she failed. Aunt

Vicky and Hannah would replace her parents. Lucas would replace BriAnn. Trees and chickens would replace restaurants and shops and the endless bustle of things happening on her street in Los Angeles.

The new version of Caitlin would replace the old Caitlin, too, but ... maybe that wasn't a bad thing, necessarily. Even with her arm in a cast, this Caitlin seemed more *herself*, somehow. Old Caitlin was always trying to be the best at everything, always trying to protect Sam, always making everyone happy.

But the *real* Caitlin didn't always want to help with the dishes.

Sam kind of liked the real Caitlin. Back home, that sort of defiance would not have gone over well.

We have to get her to the hospital.

Sam shook the voice out of her head. She got out of bed and dressed with all the speed and excitement of a girl being forced to walk the plank on a pirate ship. Aunt Vicky wanted to talk with her, and she knew exactly why.

The sky seemed on board with her impending doom. Gray clouds milled about, grumbling and threatening rain. Hopefully they'd be gone by nightfall, in time for the moon to come out. But even if they didn't, there would be magic tonight. Powerful magic. Sam could feel it.

She arrived in the kitchen at the same time Armen burst through the front door. His shirt was only partly tucked in, and strands of his hair had not been caught by his normally meticulous ponytail. Aunt Vicky handed him a cup of coffee and directed Sam to a seat at the table, where a stack of pancakes waited next to full glasses of milk and orange juice.

Aunt Vicky had made Sam breakfast.

Did she not know about Pirate Princess? But she had to! Her aunt went to bed last night, and she must have noticed that her favorite rabbit was missing.

And yet, there were pancakes. With melty butter and syrup. As if Sam deserved to eat. Sam sat and poked the pancakes with a finger. Still warm.

"Sorry I'm late," Armen said. "Miranda Ruiz called. Three of her chickens are . . ." He seemed to notice Sam for the first time and slowed down. Seemed to choose his words more carefully. "They're *missing*. Two are . . ." He hesitated again. "*Permanently* missing. One is just gone."

"Oh, poor Miranda! She loves her Rhode Island Reds," Aunt Vicky said. "What happened? Did she leave the gate open? I'll bring her something later. Maybe some extra eggs, unless you think . . . ?"

"No, that's a good idea," Armen said. "She'll probably be grief-baking for a week."

Sam stared at the table, thinking furiously. It had to be a coincidence. Missing chickens the morning after Ashander had told her to steal a chicken. Maybe chickens went missing all the time in Oregon. Maybe this had nothing to do with him.

Caitlin strolled into the room. "Lucas is outside my window

going on about paw prints and wild animals." She nodded to Armen. "He wants you to come see."

Armen raised an eyebrow at Aunt Vicky. She dropped her dish towel, and the two of them headed for the door. Sam followed, a ball of dread growing in her gut.

They hurried to the side of the house and found Lucas squatting in the tall grass.

"Dad, look!" he said, motioning to a spot on the ground.

They huddled around and stared at two large paw prints, captured perfectly in the mud just under Caitlin's open window.

Caitlin shouldered into the group next to Sam. "Is that a cat? Was it trying to get inside?"

"No, it wasn't a cat," Lucas said. "No tiny claw marks above the pads."

"A dog, then. Or a wolf," Aunt Vicky said. "They're too big to be from a fox."

"They are too big, and yet look at the position of the toes." Armen scratched his chin. "Those are definitely fox prints."

Sam hugged her arms. Ashander had been here. Outside Caitlin's window. Probably while she was sleeping.

Aunt Vicky stood up and scanned the chicken yard. Six black-and-white hens bobbed and clucked, including Lady Louise. "The chickens seem fine. Lady Louise kept them safe," she said. "But should we be worried about attacks? If there is some rogue fox on the loose . . ."

"Foxes don't attack people," Armen scoffed.

Foxes don't normally recite riddles, either, Sam thought.

She wanted to tell them. The words were sitting on her tongue. But the moment she did, it would all be over. The tests, the Golden Acorn, the way home. Everything. And then Ashander might get *really* angry.

Armen stood up and rubbed his eyes. "We're probably over-reacting. I'm very sorry for Miranda, but chickens get out of their coops all the time."

"And maybe this one just has big paws," Lucas said, poking at one of the prints.

And even bigger claws, Sam thought with a shudder.

Overhead, the skies were darkening, the clouds now an angry swirl.

"It's going to rain," Aunt Vicky said. "Let's get back inside."

Armen helped Lucas up. The four of them headed for the kitchen as the first drops of rain plunked to the earth.

Sam hesitated. Something looked wrong with the mailbox. She'd put her letter to BriAnn in there last night and lifted the flag on the side to let the mail carrier know there was a pickup.

The little flag was now missing.

She took a few steps closer. Had the mailbox always been tilted like the Leaning Tower of Pisa? No, yesterday it had been ramrod straight, perfectly perpendicular to the ground. She was sure of it.

The lid was still closed, so she tugged it open. The first drops of rain dashed themselves on her forehead.

Her letter to BriAnn was still inside. At least, pieces of it were. Someone or something had ripped it in half. She pulled out one of the scraps and recognized her drawing of a palm tree, her lies to BriAnn. A reddish-brown chicken feather clung to the back.

But none of Aunt Vicky's chickens were brown.

CHAPTER FIFTEEN

SAM SHOVED THE shredded remains of BriAnn's letter into her pocket and headed for the house. She did not look at the chickens, and especially not at Lady Louise.

Ashander's meaning was clear. Her quest wasn't just about going home anymore. Now Aunt Vicky, Hannah, and even Caitlin were in actual danger.

The trees, so high and mighty when she'd first arrived, now urged her forward with their rustling, wind-tossed limbs. *Do what must be done,* they said. *The fox's favor is worth winning.*

Inside the house, Armen and Lucas were settling into chairs at the table. Caitlin stacked wood in the fireplace, trying to coax a blaze. Aunt Vicky heated milk on the stove, an array of mismatched mugs waiting on the counter at her side.

Sam sat in front of the cooling pile of uneaten pancakes. The butter had melted in a pool at the top. The scent of maple syrup tugged at her nose. Her mother's pancakes never looked this good. Even so, she could only stomach a few bites.

Aunt Vicky handed her a mug of hot chocolate. "Are you done eating, Sam? Can we talk?"

Sam nodded, but she wanted to leap up from the table, run out the door, and keep running. She didn't even care what direction.

Instead, she followed her aunt down the hallway and into Sam's room. Aunt Vicky sat on Sam's bed, her own mug in her hands, and studied the room as if she were seeing it for the first time.

"We can paint the walls, if you want," Aunt Vicky said. She took a sip. "I don't know what your favorite color is, but I'd like to find out. Is it blue?"

Sam had been expecting any number of questions and accusations, but not this one.

"Yes, blue," she said nervously. She looked at the ring on her finger, the one she had taken from the bins. Its stone was the perfect shade.

"Excellent choice," Aunt Vicky said. She patted the bed next to her. "Sit?"

Sam hesitated. Her heart had been a wild creature all morning, frantic and unruly. Now it was trying to leap entirely out of her chest.

Even so, she did as she was told.

"My stuffed rabbit is missing," Aunt Vicky said. "But I think you already know that."

Sam sat perfectly still.

Her aunt took another sip of hot chocolate. "I don't know

why you took it, and right now, I don't care." She looked at Sam instead of her mug. "What I do care about is *you*, Sam. I care that you're hurting. I care that you're afraid. I care that you're doing all these things alone."

Pressure was building up in Sam's chest, and in her head, and behind her eyes. She could feel tears wanting to come, but did not let them. Tears were always dangerous.

I'll give you something to cry about.

Sam stared at her small library of books, now stacked on the floor by the bed. The faded spine of *The Hobbit* stared back at her.

She wanted to say, *I want my parents. I want BriAnn. I want to go home.*

But that spell didn't seem as powerful anymore.

"Change is hard, I know," Aunt Vicky said. "When I was your age, I used to pray for it. I used to beg every god I could think of—even the big one—for some sort of escape. I was so tired of trying to win love from people who awarded it like a prize. But I didn't know how to change. I didn't see any way out, and I didn't have anyone I could trust."

Sam thought of the bins of stuffed animals. Of the Queen of Squirrels. Of Pirate Princess.

Aunt Vicky started to say something. Stopped. Started again. "I want you to know that I love you, and that you can trust me. You don't have to do anything to earn these things. If you mess up, I will still love you. If you lie to me, you can still trust me. You are worthy of love, Sam. Just as you are."

The words swirled around Sam like a hurricane, a great storm of empty promises. *He'll never do it again. He loves you. He didn't mean to hurt Caitlin. This was the last time.*

The last time.

The last time.

Words were everywhere. They cost nothing to say. They changed nothing. Even if Sam wanted to believe them, how could she?

A branch slammed into the window. Sam was standing by the bed in a second, her heart racing, her legs ready to bolt.

Aunt Vicky was up just as fast, her breathing as shallow as Sam's.

"It's just the storm," Aunt Vicky said. "The window isn't even cracked. Everything is okay."

Through the glass, Sam saw a shimmer of red and purple on the edge of the forest. Not very far at all from the house.

"Everything is fine," Aunt Vicky said.

But Sam knew the truth. Everything was *not* fine.

Armen appeared in the doorway. "You okay? We heard a crash."

"A branch," Aunt Vicky said. "Scared the living daylights out of us." She put a hand over her heart and pressed, as if she could slow its beating. Sam caught herself about to do the same thing.

Did Aunt Vicky have rabbit heart, too?

Caitlin popped her head in. "What a storm, right? Maybe

we'll get thunder and lightning later! We never had anything like this in LA. I can't wait till I get to go running in the rain."

The way Caitlin grinned. The way she stood on the balls of her feet, almost bouncing in the doorway. She had never looked this happy, or this strong.

Caitlin being carried to the car in her father's arms.

Caitlin asleep in her hospital bed, so small under the white sheets.

Sam shuddered. When Sam found the Golden Acorn and they went back home . . . which Caitlin would go with her?

Armen volunteered to make the next batch of hot chocolate, and Caitlin offered to help him. The two of them headed back to the kitchen, leaving Sam with Aunt Vicky.

"We can talk again later," Aunt Vicky said. She looked as if she was going to touch Sam's arm but dropped her hand at the last minute and wiped her palms on the sides of her shorts instead. "Come to the kitchen. Your hot chocolate is cold, and we can get you a warm-up." She smiled, and Sam followed her back out to the others.

Caitlin grabbed the milk from the fridge, and Armen fiddled with the burners on the stovetop. Aunt Vicky sat down at her computer, glanced at the screen, and a rapid-fire *click-clack* of keys filled the room.

Lucas sat on the sofa, knitting. Sam quietly sat down next to him but could not stop looking over his shoulder, out the windows, toward the woods. The trees shook in the gusty wind, their branches flailing. They could not settle down. The clouds roiled above, churning in dark swirls and blotting out every last bit of sun.

Sam's brain felt like the trees looked: agitated. Restless. In constant motion.

Something blurred by the window, and Sam swore she saw Cedar's bright-yellow tunic.

"You okay?" Lucas asked. He was knitting something green and amorphous. "It looks like you're somewhere else."

"I kind of am," Sam said.

"Cool," Lucas said, and his knitting needles moved faster.

The storm gathered power as the afternoon wore on, whistling and howling against the windows and bending the trees almost in half. Sam stared out the window, hoping the squirrels were okay and wishing more than anything that tonight was not the full moon.

Armen and Lucas left early in the afternoon, worried about their walk home. Hannah's car didn't roll into the driveway until after dinner. The sky was already dark when she burst through the front door, every bit of her dripping with rain.

"Sorry I'm late! The traffic was ridiculous." She slapped the mail down on the kitchen table, where Sam was finishing her spaghetti, and let Aunt Vicky help her with her coat.

"It's wild, isn't it?" Hannah said. "I haven't seen a storm like this in years. They're expecting flash floods in the area."

Aunt Vicky hugged her, even though she was still wet. "I'm so glad you got home safe."

"It's all good, Vic, all good," Hannah said. "I sure could use some coffee, though. And is there any food left? I could eat a mountain."

"I'm on it," Aunt Vicky replied, and sped to the stove.

Sam ate the last bite of her garlic toast and looked at the pile of mail Hannah had dropped near her plate. The corner of one envelope peeked out from the stack. Sam sucked in her breath.

1172 S. Ken—

That was her home address. 1172 S. Kennington Avenue.

Sam barely moved as Hannah toweled off her hair. As Aunt Vicky put the kettle on the stove. As Caitlin bopped to her music on the sofa.

Slowly, quietly, Sam slid the letter from the stack and read the familiar perfect script:

To Samantha and Caitlin Littlefield c/o Victoria Littlefield

Her parents had written a letter.

An actual letter.

To Sam and Caitlin.

With a finger, Sam traced her own name and tried not to cry. They hadn't forgotten. They hadn't given up. They wanted Sam and Caitlin back, were desperate to reunite the family, just like Sam was. Just like Ashander promised.

We're sorry. It won't happen again. Everything's going to be okay.

Everything *was* going to be okay. How had she ever doubted? She slipped her finger under the flap of the envelope and ripped it open.

"Sam, what is that?" Aunt Vicky asked.

Too late, Sam realized her mistake. She should have stolen the letter to read later in the privacy of her room. But she'd been so eager to see what her parents said that she'd forgotten where she was.

"Sam, please," Aunt Vicky said, walking to the table and holding out her hand. "I need you to give that to me."

CHAPTER SIXTEEN

SAM SHOOK HER head and clutched the letter to her chest, not caring that she creased it. "It's addressed to me and Caitlin," Sam said. "It's our letter."

"They aren't allowed to send it to you," Aunt Vicky said. "We have to give the letter to your caseworkers. They'll read it first and decide if they can give it to you."

"But it's my letter," Sam said.

Where was Caitlin? Caitlin needed to step in and be Sam's voice. She needed to fight for them. She *always* fought for them.

Caitlin sat on the sofa, her earbuds in her hand. She wasn't smiling. "Give Aunt Vicky the letter, Sam."

Sam shook her head again, stunned. Betrayed. "Don't you want to read it? Don't you want to know?"

"I don't," Caitlin said. She cradled her cast. "I don't ever want to know."

"We can fix it. He's sorry. He'll never do it again." Sam held out the letter, so sure of the words it would contain. Words she had heard so many times.

Caitlin's eyes grew small and hot, like the embers in the fireplace. She stood up and lifted her broken arm. "This isn't like the other stuff."

The other stuff. Sam knew what Caitlin meant. *The punches. The squeezes. The pinches.*

All the things that hurt but never left a mark.

"It was a mistake," Sam said, her gaze bouncing between Hannah and Aunt Vicky and Caitlin, desperate for at least one of them to agree with her. "An accident."

Her mother had said that in the hospital. To the nurses, the doctors, the police. *It was only an accident.*

"Stop it, Sam," Caitlin said. "You don't know what I had to do to get us out of there."

Caitlin's body in her father's arms. Her mother's voice. What did you do, Grant?

"It's okay, baby," Aunt Vicky said, and this time she was talking to Caitlin, not to Sam, and she was using a soft voice. A velvet voice. No one ever talked to Caitlin like that. Caitlin was the strong child. The perfect child. The brave child. No one was supposed to feel sorry for her, not ever. Caitlin didn't let them.

Sam looked to Hannah. Hannah, who usually did most of the talking, but who had somehow fallen silent, her fingers on her lips as if to keep her words inside.

Caitlin stood stiffly by the sofa, and now she was talking

to all of them, not just to Sam. "I didn't want them to make excuses this time. I thought ..." She paused, frustrated, as she tried to find her words. "I thought, if he did something really bad ... they'd know. They'd finally know."

They. All the people who came to the hospital and asked questions. All the people who weren't in their family, who weren't *supposed* to know.

Aunt Vicky crossed the room and pulled Caitlin close, wrapped her tightly in her arms, and held her. Caitlin wasn't crying, but tears slid down Aunt Vicky's face. Tears out of nowhere. "I know," Aunt Vicky said. "I understand."

Sam waited for Caitlin to push Aunt Vicky away.

Push her away! Break the spell!

"It's going to be okay," Aunt Vicky said into Caitlin's hair. "You're safe now."

And in that moment, Sam realized that Caitlin had broken their family, and she'd done it *on purpose*. She'd pushed their father too far. She'd *wanted* to go to the hospital. She'd *wanted* the police to come. She'd *wanted* the caseworkers to ask all those horrible questions, over and over, until Sam and Caitlin had ended up on a plane to another state.

Hannah touched Sam's arm, but Sam jerked away.

"I'm sorry I startled you," Hannah said quickly. She held out her hand. "I need you to give me the letter, sweetie. Your caseworkers want to read everything first, and we need to do as they ask. We all just want to protect you and your sister."

Sam shook her head. No. *No, no, no.*

"Give it to her, Sam," Caitlin said angrily. Aunt Vicky put her hand on Caitlin's shoulder.

Sam backed away from the kitchen table. Backed away from Hannah standing with her hand out, and from Caitlin and Aunt Vicky pretending to be a family by the sofa.

How long had Sam's parents been trying to contact her?

How many letters had Hannah and Aunt Vicky stolen?

A prickly ball lodged itself in Sam's throat. Words couldn't get out, not without a lot of other stuff getting out, too. What could she do?

She could run.

She could rip open the letter and try to read it.

She could rip it up so *no one* could read it.

But such open defiance was so risky. So dangerous. It was not a thing Sam knew how to do. Hannah and Aunt Vicky had asked for the letter, and Sam had no real choice but to give it to them.

It felt like she was handing over her entire self.

"Thank you," Hannah said. She folded the letter in half and put it into her pocket. Sam watched her carefully with a storm in her eyes. Hannah patted her pocket and pulled her shirt over the top. She might as well have used a lock and key. "Hopefully I'll be able to get that back to you in a few days."

Sam clenched her fists but kept them hidden behind her back.

When she got the Golden Acorn, none of this would matter. She would fix Caitlin, and then there'd be no hospital, no Oregon, no Aunt Vicky and Hannah and Armen and Lucas. There would be no letter, because Sam would be back home with her parents the whole time.

She'd been foolish to think she could stay here, even for another night.

Outside, the storm whined and raged. The windows rattled. The trees danced with wild abandon.

The storm was not warning her. The storm was *calling* to her.

You're the hero now, not Caitlin.

She needs you. Your parents need you.

Find the Golden Acorn and make everything right.

"I want to go to my room," Sam said.

"Sam, I'm sorry," Caitlin said. Aunt Vicky's hand was still on her shoulder. "I didn't mean to be a jerk to you. Stay out here with us, Sam. We'll play a game or something. Whatever you want."

Caitlin was trying to pull Sam off course. In Greek mythology, creatures called sirens would sit on the rocks and sing to sailors, enticing them to dive off their ships and drown in the ocean. There was a time when Sam would have followed Caitlin anywhere, done whatever she asked. But not anymore.

The Golden Acorn was waiting.

A squirrel ran past the window, her blue scarf trailing after her.

"I want to go to my room," Sam said again, her voice steely.

"Go for a few minutes," Hannah said. "We'll check on you soon, and maybe then you'll want to come back out with us. Okay?"

Sam would have said anything to leave that room. "Okay" was easy. She stomped down the hallway as Aunt Vicky pulled Caitlin into another hug.

Sam knew better than to trust cottages in the forest. They were full of magic. You ate the food, you drank the hot chocolate, and then you were stuck there forever. Sam had to fight—to keep fighting—or else she might fall under the same spell that had so clearly taken Caitlin.

Before she even got to her room, Sam noticed the leaves. Piles of them, bright green and glistening with rain, and inexplicably scattered across the hallway floor, as if blown in by the wind.

She got to her room and found the window wide open, her curtains drenched. Her bedding looked soaked, too, but that wasn't what caught her eye. It was the acorns on her bedspread. Some perfect and some smashed. Dozens of them. *Hundreds.* Acorns absolutely everywhere.

Sam's hand shook as she closed her bedroom door and locked it, quick, before anyone could see.

Thunder rolled through the sky, distant and approving.

Sam emptied the pens and notebooks from her backpack onto the floor to make room for the items she might need for her quest.

A flashlight.

BriAnn's last letter, the one with all the pictures drawn on the envelope.

Her rumpled copy of *The Hobbit*.

Extra socks.

A granola bar.

The library book that would soon be overdue.

The compass Lucas had given her.

Sam's fingers lingered a moment over the compass, then she shoved it into the pack.

She pulled on Caitlin's hoodie and wished she had a raincoat to put over it. She'd almost never needed a raincoat back home, and it wasn't one of the things her mother or the caseworkers had packed for her.

Sam pulled on her boots and tugged her backpack closed.

It was time.

She tossed her backpack out the window and clambered after it.

From the Rules for Fox & Squirrels

THE HUNTING FOX

When you draw a hunting Fox from the Harvest deck and do not offer him what he wants—oh, dear!

The hunting Fox snarls and growls. He sniffs and stalks. You may barely even recognize him as the same Fox who, a few moments earlier, was so very charming.

There is no escape now. You can do nothing but stare at the Fox's fangs and wait for the sharpness of his teeth.

CHAPTER SEVENTEEN

SAM PULLED UP the hood of her sweatshirt and snuck through the yard in the darkness, the rain drenching her instantly. Inside the house, Aunt Vicky and Hannah and Caitlin sat on the sofa, their backs to the window. They hadn't heard her leaving, which meant they had no chance of seeing what she was about to do.

By the time Sam reached the chicken yard, her clothes were heavy with rain. Water dripped down her cheeks and nose, fell in big drops off her chin.

The gate to the chicken yard opened with a scratchy yawn. Sam carefully closed it behind her. There was another latch on the roof of the chicken coop. After a minute of fiddling, Sam managed to pop it off and lift the lid. A metal support folded down to keep it in place.

The chickens slept on their sturdy roost above their boxes, one next to the other, just like Aunt Vicky and Caitlin and Hannah on the sofa. They seemed so content, despite the raging storm. Lady Louise was nestled at the end, a loaf of feathers almost twice as big as the others.

Don't think about foxes, Sam told herself. *Don't think about what foxes do with chickens.*

Don't think about what happened to Pirate Princess.

She wiped her wet hands on her shorts to dry them, but her shorts were wet, too.

"I'm sorry, Lady Louise," Sam whispered. She wished there was something she could say to the chicken to make her understand, but right now, Sam wasn't sure she understood anything well enough herself.

She reached for Lady Louise with cold, shaking hands. But as soon as her fingertips brushed feathers, she yanked them back, empty.

How could she do this?

It's only a chicken. They have tiny little brains. They probably expect to be eaten by foxes.

But Lady Louise *wasn't* just a chicken. She was a living creature. With a name. And with people who loved her.

People like Aunt Vicky.

The clouds writhed overhead, but suddenly there was a break in the darkness. A single shaft of moonlight escaped the barrier and sped down to Earth, as fast as it could go. It landed on Sam and lit up the ring on her hand.

Aunt Vicky's ring.

Sam tilted the ring back and forth, letting the moonlight

catch the stone from different angles. The ring seemed to absorb the glow, seemed to suck it deep inside until a blue flame pulsed within.

It was a sign that she shouldn't sacrifice Lady Louise. Not for anyone, and not even for a quest. But then how—

"Well, well, well, what have we here?" Ashander called.

Sam spun around so fast she almost slipped. The fox strolled by outside the chicken fence, his paws clasped behind his back. The rain fell around him in sheets, but none of it seemed to touch him.

"I didn't think you would do it," he said. "I wanted you to, make no mistake, but I didn't think you would."

Behind Sam, the chickens woke and flapped their wings and squawked. They knew the fox was close, but they had nowhere to run, nowhere to hide. Sam had opened the roof of their house and exposed them to their mortal enemy.

Sam stepped in between the chickens and Ashander, trying to hide them from his view as best she could.

"I'm here, aren't I?" Sam said, sticking out her chin. She wanted his attention focused on her and not the hens. "I still have time to pass the test." If only she could figure out *how*.

"I see," Ashander said. He stalked toward her, and with every step he seemed to grow larger. By the time he stood in front of Sam—only the wire fence separating them—he was taller than her by at least a foot. "Unfortunately for you, the test has now changed."

"What? That's not fair!"

"Who said this was fair?" the fox countered. "But this is an even easier test. You'll love it, I promise!"

Sam gritted her teeth. She would *not* love it. That much was clear. She looked around for any sign of the squirrels. What happened to all the talk of no cheating? It seemed that the rules only applied to her.

"All you have to do is open this gate to the chicken yard," Ashander said. "Open the gate, and let me in."

Sam sucked in her breath. If she opened the gate just to appease him, none of the chickens would stand a chance. She remembered Aunt Vicky's face when she was talking about the neighbor's missing chickens. Aunt Vicky's face when she talked about chickens, period. Losing them would crush her.

Sam looked at her blue ring. The moonlight had sparked it to life, but the fire that burned inside it was Aunt Vicky's. Sam had the power to dampen the flame, maybe to quench it forever.

A real hero would never do that.

"Open the gate, Samantha," Ashander said, his voice sickly sweet.

Sam hated that voice. And she hated what it was trying to make her do.

"Never," she said, and she knocked out the support that kept the chicken coop's roof open. The lid slammed shut, securing the chickens inside.

Safe. They were safe. Sam sucked in a huge breath.

"That's disappointing!" the fox said. His muzzle grew longer and leaner, his teeth sharper. "And I believed you were serious about finding the Golden Acorn. With the full moon tonight, you could have wished for anything—anything at all!"

Desperation ate at her. "But you're the one who changed the test at the last minute! How am I supposed to know how to earn your favor if you're always changing what you want?"

The fox smirked. "That sounds like your problem, Samantha, not mine."

Sam stared at Ashander, at the forest, at the house, at the clouds. If only Maple and the squirrels were here. They might help find a way out of this. They knew Ashander far better than she did. Think. *Think!*

"It's a test of sacrifice," she said. "I can sacrifice something else. I have a compass. I have socks. I have books!" Even *The Hobbit*. She would even give him that.

Ashander yawned, and Sam could see every last one of his teeth.

"I can bring you fresh eggs," Sam said. Her own teeth were starting to chatter in the rain. "If you come back to Los Angeles with me, I can even bring you fresh donuts!"

Ashander picked at his claw. "You are beginning to bore me. I'd rather make my own suggestions. Perhaps I know an excellent place to find a few tasty sacrifices."

He looked up as he said it.

He looked into the house.

He looked at the figures sitting on the sofa, silhouetted against the window.

"Aunt Vicky is so trusting. She almost never locks the doors or windows," Ashander said, licking his lips. "It will be so easy to slip inside, maybe at night, when everyone is sleeping. How surprised they'll be to see me! If I give them time to be surprised at all."

Sam felt all the strength wash out of her in one great gushing wave. He was talking about Caitlin and Aunt Vicky and Hannah. *They* were the sacrifices.

She should have given him Lady Louise. If she'd only grabbed the chicken right away, then he wouldn't have asked for more. For all the chickens. For her sister. For her aunts.

Sam couldn't imagine her life without Caitlin. She was surprised to realize that she'd miss Aunt Vicky and Hannah, too. Maybe . . . maybe even a lot.

This was her fault. All of it. She'd wanted to save her family, but now that word—*family*—was starting to mean something a little different.

There was only one thing left to try.

Sam swallowed the lump in her throat and tried to steady her voice. "I'll be the sacrifice," she said. "Take me, and leave my family alone."

Ashander threw back his head and laughed.

"Oh, Sam! I knew you weren't the selfish child that everyone said you were! You have finally cast aside your petty wants and needs, and are looking at the bigger picture." He gripped the fence between them, his claws poking through the mesh. "You are finally looking at what *I* want and need."

The fox's eyes had gone dark and hard, and she had seen them before. *So many times before.* A dank chill worked its way through Sam's body, freezing her from the inside out.

"Come out of the chicken yard, Samantha," Ashander said quietly. "Let us see that you pass this final test."

What had she done? What could she do?

Her mother's voice.

What have you done? Oh, God, what have you done?

In the distance, a strange animal howled high and bright. It was no animal Sam had ever heard before.

Ashander's ears swiveled toward the noise. His long nose sniffed the air. "Stay in your cage, little chicken," he snarled. "I will be right back."

The fox dropped to all four feet, and he was now as big as a wolf. He bounded into the forest in one great leap, his purple coat snapping like thunder.

Sam barely waited for him to disappear before she bolted out of the chicken yard, securing the gate behind her. She glanced at the house. Hannah was at the kitchen sink, but Aunt Vicky and Caitlin were still on the sofa, blissfully unaware of the danger they were in.

Even if Ashander took Sam as a sacrifice, he might go after

Caitlin next. Even if he promised not to. Ashander kept chang-ing the rules. There was no pleasing him, and definitely no trusting him.

Rain pelted her from above, wind buffeted her from the sides. She was suddenly grateful for the ground, which did nothing but stay firm and hold her up.

Sam touched the blue stone on her ring. A prick of warmth shot through her finger. There was magic in it still.

And there was still fight in Sam.

She dug the compass and the flashlight from her bag. She'd wanted the Golden Acorn to take her back home, but now she needed that wish for something more important: to stop Ashander and protect the people she loved. And since the fox was no longer helping her—had maybe never been helping her—then she'd have to find the Golden Acorn herself.

FROM THE RULES FOR FOX & SQUIRRELS

PLANNING FOR THE FOX

You can try to plan for the Fox. You can save up your cards for him instead of trying to prepare for winter. Many people do. They spend so much time worried about the Fox that they forget about the rest of the game entirely.

But remember: you never know when the Fox will appear, or what kind of Fox he will be when he does.

And by then, it will be too late.

CHAPTER EIGHTEEN

ACCORDING TO THE compass, Ashander had raced northwest. Sam shouldered her backpack and ran northeast. Even if she couldn't find the Golden Acorn, at least she'd be leading Ashander away from Caitlin and her aunts.

The forest loomed before her, more shadow than tree. She reached its border and plunged inside. Night had fallen hard and heavy, and it was almost pitch-black in the grip of the trees. Her backpack whacked her in the spine repeatedly because she hadn't taken the time to tighten the straps. She kept her flashlight moving left and right and back again so she wouldn't run headlong into a tree trunk or blind herself on an errant branch.

"We're here!" a squirrel voice said.

Sam swung the flashlight and found Maple and Cedar running beside her. Maple wore a raincoat of shiny, bright-blue fabric with the oversized hood pulled up to shield her ears. Cedar wore yellow galoshes on all four of his paws.

"Where's Birch?" Sam asked, ducking under the sticky branch of a pine.

Maple did not answer immediately, panting as she ran. "Birch volunteered to distract Ashander so you could escape. Perhaps you heard her howl."

"Oh, no," Sam said. She grew panicked picturing Birch with her tiny sword, trying to fend off a fox. "Is she okay?"

Is she okay? Mom, is she okay?

"We don't know," Cedar said.

"We will hope that she is," Maple replied firmly. "Birch is strong."

The forest blurred, and for a moment Sam couldn't tell if she was stumbling between tree trunks in the middle of a storm or navigating an endless hospital hallway that flickered in and out in time with its fluorescent lights. *Caitlin will wake up, Sam. She will. She's strong.*

"He wouldn't hurt her, would he?" Sam asked in a small voice.

Maple ran silently. "Not on purpose, but ... maybe by accident."

It was an accident.

"Why would she do that for me?" The rain was everywhere, even in her eyes. Sam wiped them with her soaking sleeve. "I never asked her to do that!"

"Do you mean Birch or Caitlin?" Maple asked.

"I meant ..."

But suddenly Sam didn't know how to answer. When she pictured Birch, the squirrel had a cast on her foreleg. When she pictured Caitlin, her sister was wearing a knight's helmet and brandishing a sword made of sticks.

Maple slid to a stop. Cedar nearly collided into her.

"Quiet. Ashander is in the forest," Maple said.

Sam peered into the dark behind them and tried to silence her rasping breaths. "How close?"

"It's hard to tell," Maple said. "The wind is being coy with his scent."

"The trees are letting him pass," Cedar said, hugging his arms to his chest. He wasn't wearing his galoshes anymore—just his normal yellow tunic and pants, already soaked from the rain.

"We still don't know where to find the Golden Acorn," Sam said. She shined the flashlight on the compass. They were still headed northeast, but who knew if that was even right. Ashander was going to catch her before she found it.

Sam switched the flashlight off to save the battery. As her eyes adjusted to the dark, a strange thing happened: the directions and hands of the compass lit up as if Sam had plugged them into a light switch. A glow-in-the-dark compass! Why hadn't Lucas mentioned that when he gave it to her?

Maybe because Sam was too busy throwing it at him.

She studied the compass and noticed something odd. The regular compass hand and ordinal directions weren't visible in the darkness, but a new, glowing symbol had appeared, along with a glowing arrow. They must have been hidden under the glare of the flashlight.

Wait, Sam thought. Somewhere up above the trees and the clouds, there was a full moon. It was the *moon* that had turned Lucas's compass to magic. Sam peered closer, hoping to see what her heart most desired.

The symbol was an *acorn*.

Her compass could direct her to the Golden Acorn!

"Look, look!" Sam knelt and held out the compass so Maple and Cedar could see. "That symbol represents the Golden Acorn. All we have to do is turn until the arrow points to it, and then we know we're going in the right direction!"

"How marvelous," Maple said, clapping her paws. "You are such a clever girl, Samantha."

Sam's chest swelled with something other than panic for a change.

Cedar turned and sniffed the air. "I can smell him." He looked at Sam, his eyes wide and afraid. "Ashander is *hunting*."

"We should move quickly," Maple said. She touched Cedar's shoulder, and he shivered. Maple took off her raincoat and wrapped it around the younger squirrel. The blue fabric turned yellow the moment she buttoned it.

"If things get ugly, I will do what I can to protect you," Maple said. She looked up at Sam. "And you, too, Samantha. I will do everything in my power."

Sam stared into Maple's determined eyes and couldn't coax a single word from her own throat. She nodded gratefully.

"Now lead us to the Golden Acorn, Sam," Maple said. "We haven't much time!"

Sam turned until the glowing compass arrow lined up with the acorn symbol. "This way."

The forest had never been silent, but now it was a raging cacophony. Branches snapped, leaves rustled, rain drummed against every surface. Animals darted through the underbrush and leaped from tree to tree overhead. Sam's clothes were twice as heavy now that they were soaked with water, and despite the summer month, it grew colder every minute. Soon her breath came in ragged puffs.

Sam stopped to check the compass. Had she been gone five minutes, or ten minutes, or three hours? Aunt Vicky's house felt as far away as Oz or Narnia or middle-earth.

"I'm done," Cedar said, huffing at Sam's side. "I don't want to do this anymore."

"Shush now," Maple said, patting him on the back. She seemed only mildly winded by their run and had somehow acquired another blue raincoat. "You don't mean that."

"I do mean it," Cedar said angrily. "We had everything fig-ured out before *she* got here. We knew his moods. We knew what to say and what not to say. We knew when to lower our eyes or to laugh or to fetch him his dinner. He liked my juggling—it made him smile once! He only got angry sometimes, and only when we deserved it. Everything would have kept on being okay if she hadn't come to the forest." He glared at Sam. "You ruined everything!"

"*Shh, shh,*" Maple said.

Sam couldn't help feeling hurt. Didn't Cedar see how manipulative Ashander was? How the fox slid between happy and angry and tricky and sweet so fast that there was no way to keep up? How Ashander said one thing but did another?

"It's not my fault that he's like that," Sam said. "It's not my fault that you have to worry so much about what he's thinking."

"The forest was better before you got here," Cedar said.

"That's enough," Maple said sternly. "We have no time for this bickering."

"If you don't want to stay, then don't," Sam told Cedar. "I'm not making you do something you don't want to do."

Cedar crossed his arms. "If I have a choice, then I'm definitely leaving. And I think you should turn around, too. It doesn't help anyone to go against Ashander's wishes. You should give yourself up and beg for forgiveness. He'll punish all of us if you don't!"

"If you're going to leave, then go," Maple said crossly.

"Fine, I will. And if you're smart, you'll go too, Maple." Cedar gave Sam one last defiant glare, then darted into the night.

The compass shook in Sam's hand. She tried to focus on its face instead of on the disappearing tail of a squirrel she'd thought was her friend.

"You may as well go, too," Sam said to the compass, because she couldn't bring herself to look at Maple.

"Of course I'm staying," Maple said. "I promised to protect you, and I will."

"Thank you, Maple." Sam wiped her nose with her very wet sleeve. "I wish Ashander stayed charming."

Maple's determined face grew sad. She touched Sam's leg with her paw. "Nobody is only one thing."

"Then I wish he weren't charming at all. If he hadn't been so nice at the beginning, if I didn't like him, then it wouldn't matter so much that, that . . ."

"That he's hunting us," Maple said.

"Yeah."

"Let's run, child," the squirrel said, and they did.

The farther they went into the forest, the darker it got. Sam tripped over a tree root and landed face-first in the mud. Her body ached. Maple cleaned the muck from Sam's eyes and got her back on her feet. They kept running, but this time with the flashlight. It was impossible to know how far they had to go. The compass told them the direction, but not the distance. The Golden Acorn might still be miles away.

Strange voices echoed through the forest. Sam couldn't tell what they were saying, not through the noise of the rain. It was like a thousand drummers were banging on the leaves and the tree trunks and the ground, determined to be as loud as possible.

A twig snapped, and Sam swung the flashlight.

Nothing.

She swept it in the other direction, and a dark shape darted away from the beam.

"He's close," Maple said. "Faster!"

Sam sped up, but her boots slid in the mud. She fell to her hands and knees. The flashlight dropped from her grip and rolled away, the beam bouncing wildly.

Maple tugged at Sam's hand. "Get up! Get the flashlight! We have to go!"

Sam tried to stand, but her shoes kept slipping and her hands were so numb that they refused to do what she asked. Plus, she was sure that her left shin was bleeding from the fall.

A howl cut through the darkness, silencing both the rain and the voices.

Sam scrambled forward, but all she managed to do was twist and land on her rear in what felt like a stream. The water was freezing! At least she got her almost useless fingers to wrap around the flashlight.

And there, in the spotlight of her beam, was Ashander.

His purple coat had ripped along its seams. Mud matted the fur of his arms and legs. But he leaned against a tree trunk and studied his claws, as if he'd been casually waiting for her the whole time.

Chapter Nineteen

"*MY, MY, MY*, what have we here?" said the fox with a sly smile. His eyes grew big. "Why, it's the sacrifice!"

Sam scuttled backward like a crab.

Ashander chuckled. "I do so love a good hunt, but I'm sure you know that the punishment is always so much worse when you try to outrun it."

"Please, no," Maple said, wringing her paws. "She'll bring you the chicken. All the chickens. She'll do whatever you ask. Promise him, Sam. Promise him!"

Sam could barely feel her fingers or her toes. Her teeth chattered. Every last bit of her was drenched. But she would promise no such thing. Ashander could not be trusted. Promising him the world might keep her safe tonight, but it would mean nothing tomorrow.

"Please, Samantha!" Maple begged. She stood between Sam and Ashander with her arms outstretched, as if she could stop them both with her tiny paws. "Do not anger him further!"

"You're wasting your breath," Ashander snarled. In a flash, his humor and wit vanished. Rather, Sam *wished* they had vanished. The aspects she loved were probably all still there, still every bit a part of him. Knowing this—that he could be this fox and the other fox at the same time—only made him more terrifying.

Ashander stalked toward Maple. "Unless you want to find out exactly how sharp my teeth are, you'd better fall in line yourself."

Maple recoiled. "I'm sorry, I'm sorry, I'm sorry!"

Sam doubted Maple even knew why she was apologizing. Those words had been spoken so often in Sam's house, repeated over and over like a protection spell. Only, it rarely worked.

"Maple isn't part of this," Sam said, desperate. "It's my fault, not hers!"

Ashander ignored Sam. "Oh, so you remember my teeth, do you," he said to Maple. He smiled, and it was the most awful thing Sam had ever seen. "I'll make this simple. It's you or Samantha, Maple dear. Choose wisely, or you know what will happen. You know how bad it will be."

Sam held her breath. All she could do was watch Maple's small face and hope.

The moment Maple decided, her bright eyes dulled and her slender shoulders rounded. She always stood so tall and perfect, but now she shrank, as if all the life had leaked out of her.

Sam knew what was coming next. What always came next. *I'm sorry, Grant. I won't do it again.*

"Samantha made me come with her," Maple said, her voice flat. "She always intended to defy you."

Sam's eyes filled, but not with rain. Her lip trembled, but not from the cold.

"Aaaaaah," Ashander said, stalking closer. "I thought as much! Such a selfish girl. Weak and helpless."

Sam barely heard him. She could not stop staring at Maple, even though she could barely see the squirrel through all the useless water falling from her eyes.

I'll do what I can to protect you.

Those were the words Maple had said.

I'll do what I can to protect you.

But Maple had given Sam up to save herself. She'd handed Sam to the fox without a fight.

The fox would have hurt Maple. He had obviously hurt her before. But even so, Sam wanted . . .

She wished . . .

She hoped . . .

That maybe this time, Maple would have loved her enough to at least *try*.

Sam watched as Maple walked slowly to Ashander's side and looked up at him with terrified eyes. He patted her on the head. "Good girl, Maple. You did the right thing."

Maple did not relax, not even a little. Her shoulders

remained stiff, her tail twitched. Every time the fox moved, Maple flinched.

"Run along home now, Maple," Ashander said gently. "I've no quarrel with you. Not tonight."

Maple dropped her head, defeated. She didn't even look at Sam again as she fell to her four paws and bounded into the shadows.

"It's just you and me now, Samantha. That's the way it always should have been, don't you think?" the fox said, suddenly charming again. "You are such a clever girl. So much smarter than the others."

Sam wiped her eyes furiously. She hated how his words made her feel. She hated how much she wanted to believe them. But she could see the fangs in his mouth for what they were.

Ashander's tail swished. "The test of sacrifice, Sam. You still need to pass it. After I'm done with you, I might just climb the gate to the chickens for fun. Who'll be there to stop me?"

Sam refused to give up like this, not when so many people still needed her. Not when she was so close to the Golden Acorn. But how could she escape long enough to find it?

Maybe it was time for her to start changing the rules, too.

The fox stalked closer, drawing out his approach. Trying to make her more afraid. Good. Sam whispered words under her breath, searched for rhymes, tested syllables. Why didn't *orbit* rhyme with anything? There was no time to invent something elaborate, but then again, in *The Hobbit* when Bilbo had needed a riddle, he'd simply asked, "What have I got in my pocket?" Sam could at least do better than that!

When Ashander was almost upon her, she held up her hand, as if she could stop his approach with just her five fingers and the ring Aunt Vicky had let her keep.

"Oh, little one, do you really think your small paw could stop me?" the fox asked. "How foolish!"

"I've promised you a sacrifice, but you must earn it," Sam said, pleased when her voice didn't waver. "You must answer my riddle."

As Sam spoke those words, the forest around them lit up, as if someone was flicking the light switch to the sun. Thunder shook the trees.

Ashander laughed. "The lightning was a nice touch. A bit dramatic, but suitable for the occasion. However, there is absolutely no reason why I should have to do anything you ask, my tasty little sacrifice."

Sam cried out as the ring on her finger burst into blue flames. But it didn't hurt—in fact, a comforting warmth rushed through her arm and wrapped around her chest. It almost felt like being *hugged*.

Ashander stepped back with a hiss. "Well, this is unexpected."

Aunt Vicky's words came back to Sam: *There are a lot of dangers in these woods. You might need the queen's magic.*

The ring wasn't just Aunt Vicky's ring; it had belonged to the Queen of Squirrels!

Ashander tried to recover his ground, but the ring flared brighter. He stayed where he was. "Fine. Tell me your riddle, then. I am excellent at solving puzzles and was going to ask for it anyway."

Sam almost had the words in the right order. Almost. It was so hard to think when she was so cold, and so scared. She took a deep breath, counted to five, and spoke:

Above the mountains, seas, and cities
A lady drifts in shadowed air
Smiling
Frowning
Hiding
Howling
But always, ever there.

Her ring blazed, casting Sam, Ashander, and a million drops of rain in eerie blue light. She hadn't done anything, not on purpose. Had her words activated hidden magic in the ring, like some kind of spell?

Ashander tried to take a step forward but grunted and twisted in place, the first ungraceful move she'd seen him make.

He growled. "Oh, you've bound me to the answer, have you? I can't move until I solve it? Clever, Samantha. Clever!" He tried to grin, tried to seem at ease despite his legs being literally stuck to the ground. "Very well, then, I will solve your little riddle. It's probably something ridiculous, like an owl or a human hanging from a tree."

Wrong, Sam thought, but she didn't waste time saying it. She pulled out her compass—careful not to look at her watch, lest she give Ashander a clue—adjusted her bearing, and ran.

Ashander called after her. "Is it a witch on a broomstick? Is it a moth?"

The good news was that Ashander was not particularly good at riddles. The bad news was that he was guessing so much that he'd stumble upon the actual answer before too long.

Sam could not run very fast. Her legs ached. Her bones shivered. Her fingers were so numb that she could barely hold on to the compass and the flashlight while still making sure she didn't poke her eyes out on a sharp branch. Every last bit of her was dripping. It would be so much easier if she just sat down in the mud and closed her eyes. Was it like this for all heroes, near the end?

The blue ring flared again, and Sam pushed those thoughts aside. The Queen of Squirrels was lending her strength. She would not squander it.

"Is it a chicken trying to fly?"

"Is it a jack-o'-lantern?"

Ashander's guesses followed her through the woods, and even though he was still stuck in place, the ominous threat of his voice never grew distant. She could almost feel his warm breath on her cheek.

"Is it a face on a tree?"

The compass took Sam left and right, matching the twists and turns of a creek. When she'd fallen earlier, it had barely been more than a puddle. Now it was a full-on stream, rushing past her ankles as she tromped along its shore.

"Is it a candle flame?" asked Ashander's voice in her ear.

The ring continued to cast a light around Sam as if she were traveling in a warm blue spotlight. The Queen of Squirrels had worn this ring on her tail, but it was also Aunt Vicky's ring. Aunt Vicky had crowned the queen in the first place.

There are a lot of dangers in these woods, her aunt had said. She must have known that from experience.

"Is it a porch light?" the fox guessed.

Sam tried to speed up, yanking her boots from the greedy mud with each step. On the compass, the acorn symbol began to pulse faster. Did that mean she was getting closer? Was she almost there?

Ashander whispered in her ear, "Is it the moon?"

Sam gasped. The glow on her ring winked out.

Ashander had spoken the true answer.

The moon. Smiling and frowning described its crescent phases, the full moon was it howling, and it was "hidden" when it was new, not visible in the "shadowy" night sky. But it was always there, no matter what face it was showing. Even now, when it was trapped above the trees and the clouds, she could feel it.

"The moon, Sam, the moon! What a clever girl. I could have guessed that right away, if I'd wanted," Ashander said, from wherever he was. "But now I'm coming for you. I'll be there before you can find anywhere to hide."

But Sam had no intention to hide.

Now it was a *race*.

Up the slippery bank of the creek she stumbled, her boots threatening to come off with each slurpy step. She tried not to think about Birch or Cedar or Maple and what had become of them. Instead, she pictured BriAnn and Lucas on either side of her, lifting her from the muck every time it tried to swallow her.

"Saa-aaam," Ashander sang. "Why don't you stop and wait for me, Sam? I'll give you a new test. An easy test. And then we'll find the Golden Acorn together."

Lies, all lies! Or, at least, half-truths.

Everything about that fox was changeable. His words, his promises, his moods. Sam had wanted to please him, to earn his favor, but how could she when what he wanted never stayed the same? Her aunt's words came back to her: *I was so tired of trying to win love from people who awarded it like a prize.* Well, Sam was done with prizes, and she was done with games.

"Sam!" voices called in the distance. "Saa-aaam!"

Of course Ashander would bring friends. Maybe they were more foxes, or even wolves. Well, he could set the whole forest after her if he wanted, and it would make no difference. The only path was forward.

The forest grew brighter. Sam pushed through a thicket and saw a shaft of clear moonlight shining down through the trees ahead of her, illuminating a clearing.

The compass was sure: she'd found the Golden Acorn.

From the Rules for
Fox & Squirrels

WINNING

In most games, the person with the most points at the end is the winner. But this is a game of Fox & Squirrels, and it's not just about winning.

Fox & Squirrels is about survival.

Survive the fox.

Survive the winter.

SURVIVE.

Sometimes survival is all you can think about. That's okay. Really.

Survival is important.

It's the only way you get to play Fox & Squirrels again.

CHAPTER TWENTY

A MASSIVE, CRACKED tree trunk dominated the center of the clearing like a jagged throne, its roots covered in a skirt of vines and pine cones. Glowing runes spiraled over its bark, written in a language Sam had never seen. The language of foxes or squirrels, or maybe the language of the forest itself.

But Sam's gaze was drawn upward, to the tallest splinter of wood jutting from the top of the trunk. Balanced atop this spike and bathed in moonlight sat the Golden Acorn.

Sam gasped. Even two dozen feet away, it was the most beautiful sight she had ever seen. A part of her had wondered if the Golden Acorn was even real, if maybe it was just another lie Ashander had told her. But her heart had believed, and here it was. Sam had been brave enough to find it, after all.

The Golden Acorn tugged at Sam, urged her forward, pulled at her in every way short of calling her name.

"What's this? Does our little Samantha see something she wants?"

Ashander stood on the other side of the clearing, already on all fours. His purple coat had reformed into sleek leather armor. He growled, and the hairs on the back of Sam's neck raised.

"You can't have the Golden Acorn," Ashander said. "You don't *deserve* the Golden Acorn."

"I deserve it more than you do," Sam snarled back.

The fox crouched, his muscles bunching. He was preparing to pounce.

She'd seen the documentaries. She knew how high foxes could jump, and how precisely they could land, teeth gnashing.

This was it, then.

The last battle.

Sam squared her shoulders, determined to try her hardest. Had Caitlin felt like this on that night, when she faced their father? The forest disappeared for a moment, and Sam was standing in the hallway outside Caitlin's room while her mother pounded on the door. Sam's toes dug into the carpet. Maybe, that night, Caitlin hadn't wanted to say *I'm sorry* for the hundredth time. Maybe she'd said to herself instead, *Let him snarl. Let him snap.*

"Sam!"

The voice cut through the darkness, so loud that even Ashander turned to look.

A few days ago, Aunt Vicky's voice had reminded Sam of a fluttering moth, easy to miss. But this was Aunt Vicky, too. Piercing, strong. Was her aunt in the woods? Was she trying to rescue Sam?

"She won't save you," Ashander said. He wore an eyepatch now and a big hoop earring. One of his fangs glinted silver, like a pirate. "She never asked for you or your sister to come here. She doesn't want you. She doesn't care about you."

I want you to know that I love you.

Sam knew that the minute she stepped into the light of the clearing, the fox would be on her. She had to be ready. She had to be fast.

"The squirrels abandoned you. Your aunt will leave you, too," Ashander said, pacing along the edge of the light. "All you've done is disappoint her. You've taken her things, and you've broken them. It's only a matter of time before she throws you out . . . or worse."

You can trust me.

Sam dropped the compass and the flashlight. She tossed her backpack into the mud. She bolted into the light.

The fox crouched.

Sam ran as hard as she could, but she wasn't Caitlin. She wasn't fast enough. She kept running anyway.

Ashander sprang, claws flashing.

The Golden Acorn was too far away. Too far!

Sam raised her arm to ward off Ashander's teeth. He

tackled her to the ground, and she rolled, trying to shake him off while he clawed and bit. His mouth opened wide—Sam could have counted his teeth—and he sank his fangs into her arm.

Only . . . the moment before his canines ripped through Caitlin's hoodie and into Sam's flesh, the sweatshirt changed. Blue light rippled over the fabric, and in its wake, the simple cotton transformed into shining metal.

It was Caitlin's sweatshirt. She had given Sam her own suit of armor.

Ashander bit into Sam's metal sleeve and yowled in pain. His claws scrabbled at her chest, but the armor repelled them.

Sam shoved the fox away and vaulted to her feet. Ashander was right behind her. She lunged for the Golden Acorn, hand grasping. Her fingers wrapped around something smooth and round and heavy. She squeezed.

The Golden Acorn!

Ashander tackled her again.

Sam curled up to protect herself. The hoodie covered most of her, but her legs were exposed, and her feet, and her face. Ashander was on her now, teeth bared. Sam thrashed and tried to throw him off.

"Sam, where are you?" Aunt Vicky called, but her voice was growing fainter instead of louder. She was going in the wrong direction.

If you mess up, I will still love you.

Ashander sank his fangs into Sam's leg, and she yelped.

If you lie to me, you can still trust me.

"Aunt Vicky," Sam cried, but the night swallowed up her voice in one easy gulp, as if she hadn't said anything at all.

Ashander laughed. "Pathetic." He snarled and snapped at her again.

Sam needed her voice. Her mouth gaped, but nothing came out. *Don't talk. Don't tell. Don't trust.* Years of unspoken words were lodged in Sam's throat.

Ashander's paws pressed her into the ground. He looked down at her and growled, "Don't say a word."

Sam stared into the fox's cold, charming, warm, angry eyes and heard other words.

You are worthy of love, Sam. Just as you are.

Sam yelled.

She yelled as loud as she could.

She used her lungs and her heart and every last thing she could find inside herself.

"Help! Aunt Vicky! The fox is on me! The fox!"

"Quiet!" Ashander growled. "No one cares what happens to you."

Sam imagined Aunt Vicky crashing through the forest, fighting off twisting vines with a sword and dodging lightning. She imagined Aunt Vicky emerging from the darkness and challenging Ashander to a duel. She imagined Aunt Vicky—

And then, amid cracking branches, Aunt Vicky herself erupted from the darkness, swinging a sword of light.

The real Aunt Vicky.

Sam had called for her, and she'd come.

Aunt Vicky spotted Sam and charged, knocking Ashander away as if he wasn't even there. He hissed and shrank down to normal fox size. Maybe even smaller. The vicious spark in his eyes dimmed but did not go out. He slunk into the shadows with his wet, ratty tail between his legs.

Suddenly there were fingers around Sam's arms. There were warm hands pulling her up, off the ground. Away from the cold. Away from the fox.

"Sam, say something," Aunt Vicky said. "Oh, God, you're soaked and freezing." She held Sam against her with one arm and waved the flashlight with her other hand. "I found her! I found her!"

"Ashander tried to stop me, but I found the Golden Acorn," Sam tried to say. Her lips were thick and numb, and it came out all wrong. She could barely keep her hand closed tight. "I get to make a wish. I get to fix everything."

Aunt Vicky lifted Sam into her arms and wrapped her raincoat around them both. The rain clattered angrily at the fabric but couldn't get through.

"Pirate Princess and the mouse and almost Lady Louise," Sam sobbed.

"It's okay. I understand. I really do," Aunt Vicky said. "Oh,

Sam." Aunt Vicky's arms were around her, holding Sam so tight she could barely move. Which was okay, actually. Sam didn't want to move. Not even when she realized her aunt was crying, too.

"The fox . . . ," Sam said.

"The fox is gone. Do you hear me? It's gone," Aunt Vicky said. "I won't let it hurt you. I won't let anyone hurt you."

Sam thought about Ashander's eyepatch and hoop earring, just like the ones that were on Aunt Vicky's stuffed animal pirates. Aunt Vicky *did* understand. And if Aunt Vicky understood, maybe she could actually do what she promised.

Inside Sam's chest, her heart gave a timid, hopeful rabbit thump.

Hannah and Caitlin arrived, breathless, and took turns hugging Sam.

"You jerk," Caitlin said, and hugged Sam harder. "I gave you my hoodie, and this is what you do with it? It's not water-resistant!"

"You're not supposed to get your cast wet," Sam said, because she didn't know how to say, *It's good to see you, too.*

Caitlin pushed wet hair away from her eyes and grinned. "Worth it."

Sam didn't dare open her fingers to look at the Golden Acorn, but she could feel it there, pressed against her palm like the pit at the center of an avocado. Aunt Vicky helped her walk all the way back to the house. Hannah volunteered to carry her, but Sam refused. She wanted to walk. It seemed important. It seemed like something a hero would do. She'd gone into the woods, and now she was leaving them. *There and back again.*

Ashander did not follow or attack.

They were four now, and he was only one fox.

FROM THE RULES FOR FOX & SQUIRRELS

HOUSE RULE #1: PLAYERS CAN WORK TOGETHER

When the Fox arrives, all players can contribute cards to soothe him, and at the end of the game, all points are totaled to see if everyone survives winter together.

Oh, it's much easier now? OF COURSE IT IS.

That's what friends do.

That's what family is.

No one is ever alone.

CHAPTER TWENTY-ONE

SAM PRESSED THE phone to her ear, nervous. Aunt Vicky had already talked to BriAnn's parents, but Sam hadn't yet talked to BriAnn. What if she was angry? What if she was sad? What if she didn't believe any of the things Aunt Vicky had told her parents about why Sam and Caitlin moved to Oregon?

"Hello?" a voice said.

"BriAnn? It's me, Sam." She was rewarded with BriAnn's squeal.

"Saaaaaam! I missed you so much! You have to tell me everything about Oregon, okay? Everything! How soon can I visit? My mom said she's always wanted to visit Portland, and she can bring me. I've already researched all the animals I want to draw, like a beaver and a Steller's jay! And you can introduce me to all your new friends, too."

Sam grinned into the mouthpiece. "Well, there's only the one friend now, Lucas, unless you count Aunt Vicky and Hannah. They're old, but they're nice."

Across the room, at the kitchen table, Hannah laughed. Sam liked the sound.

"Sam, I totally get why you didn't want to tell me you were moving," BriAnn said in her serious voice. "There's stuff I find hard to talk about, too."

"There is?" Sam asked. She thought BriAnn told her everything, and it hurt a little to know that she didn't.

Which . . . was kind of BriAnn's point, Sam realized.

"So we make a pact to tell each other stuff," Sam said. The idea made her heart a little fluttery, but maybe in a good way.

"Deal!" BriAnn said instantly. "I have to tell you about this guy my mom met at the wedding. I actually caught them kissing!"

Sam pressed the phone to her ear, eager to hear every word. Clearly BriAnn was already better at sharing stuff, but Sam could catch up. She could do anything.

By the time she and BriAnn hung up, they had plans to see each other, pending BriAnn's mother's schedule and miscellaneous stuff, like school. It was something, at least. And BriAnn promised to send more pictures in her letters, to tide Sam over.

Sam still hadn't gotten the letter that her parents had sent, but Mr. Sanchez said he'd have a new one for her soon. There were rules to be followed, and unlike Ashander, Mr. Sanchez didn't change them.

"Who's up for a game?" Aunt Vicky asked.

"Me!" Lucas said instantly. He put away his knitting and leaped over to the kitchen table. "But not Monopoly. My dad said it glamorizes the real estate market."

Aunt Vicky snorted.

Caitlin removed an earbud. "Game time? I'm in. I need revenge."

"I'll get the rhubarb pie and ice cream," Hannah said. "If you monsters left any of it after lunch," she added.

Sam paused on her way to the table and looked out the window. It was easy to spot Birch playing high up in the branches. Nowadays, she and the Queen of Squirrels were inseparable, always adventuring together, always watching each other's backs. Sam wouldn't be surprised if the queen knighted Birch before too long. Sam only hoped they would invite her to the ceremony.

She turned away from the window. "Can we try Fox and Squirrels?" She'd had the game for almost two weeks now, and she still hadn't played for real.

Aunt Vicky pumped her arm in some sort of victory maneuver. It was super dorky.

Hannah rolled her eyes. "It's only her favorite game of all time. Did she pay you to suggest it, Sam?"

"Not this time," Sam laughed.

Aunt Vicky wiped the table while Sam got the game from her room. Lucas reached for the cards, oohing and aahing over the artwork. When he exclaimed over one of the fox cards, Sam shuddered. She couldn't help it. The fox on the card looked so much like Ashander.

"Do you know what house rules are?" Aunt Vicky asked. She sat down next to Sam and held out her hand for the cards. Lucas gave them to her.

Sam shook her head. "House rules?"

"Yep." Aunt Vicky shuffled through the cards with practiced ease, pulling out all the foxes and putting them in their own separate pile, lickety-split. "Sometimes you figure out a way to change the game so that it's more fun, and you play with those rules instead of the official ones."

Sam snaked her hand under the table and into the pocket of her shorts. The Golden Acorn was still there, smooth and cool. She kept it with her every day, and had developed the habit of touching it to prove to herself that it was still there.

Her new therapist, Dr. Beranek, said keeping the Acorn was okay. Dr. Beranek said a lot of things, but mostly just listened while Sam did the talking.

"Does this game have any house rules?" Lucas asked.

Sam already knew the answer. She'd read the rules over and over, though she'd never known that it was Aunt Vicky's handwriting at the end. And she hadn't known enough about the game to understand what Aunt Vicky's rules meant.

"I've got a few to suggest," Aunt Vicky said. "But we won't use them unless everyone agrees. And before that can happen, I have to explain how to play." She shuffled the deck—without the fox cards—and started to deal. "This first round will just be practice."

"But after that, all bets are off," Hannah said, pulling out the chair next to Lucas. "I'm terrible at cards, but I love to win!"

Sam touched the Acorn again.

The morning after her showdown with Ashander in the woods, she'd been surprised to find the Golden Acorn still in her palm. Aunt Vicky must have seen it when she helped Sam get changed for bed, but she never said anything. Sam was surprised, too, that the Golden Acorn wasn't actually golden. It was a dull grayish brown, a lot like a plain old river rock.

At first she'd panicked, thinking she hadn't found the Golden Acorn after all. But later, she realized the truth: once you found the Acorn and got your wish, the color faded. The magic was gone.

No, not gone. *Used up.*

Sam had read enough stories to know that wishes were persnickety. They didn't always do what you *thought* you wanted. Sometimes they looked into your soul and gave you what you *really* wanted instead.

"Okay, pick up your cards," Aunt Vicky said. "The goal of the game is to collect enough nuts to survive the winter. We're going to do that by collecting cards—"

"I'm already confused," Lucas said, but he didn't look the least bit upset by the revelation. "Can I play as a squirrel?"

Aunt Vicky started to answer, but Sam beat her to it.

"Yes, you can play as a squirrel," Sam said. Everyone looked at her, even Caitlin. And they waited for her to keep talking. "I mean, if everyone agrees. Then we'll make it a house rule. Anyone who wants to play as a squirrel gets to be a squirrel. That's how it works, right?"

Aunt Vicky beamed. "That's exactly how this family works."

From the Rules for Fox & Squirrels

HOUSE RULE #2: REMOVE ALL THE FOX CARDS

The Fox can be sweet. The Fox can be charming. The Fox can seem like the center of the universe. But the truth is that when you play with the Fox, everything is ABOUT THE FOX.

It is far, far better to make the game about you.

Remove the Fox. Go on. Turn the cards upside down, put them at the bottom of the box, or throw them out, if you want.

See how much easier it is to survive winter when you aren't glancing over your shoulder all the time. When you aren't worrying about what he'll do.

Notice how you actually start looking forward to spring.

AUTHOR'S NOTE

This is the book I always knew I had to write. My own story is not unusual; in fact, maybe it's your story, too. Maybe you live with someone who makes you feel afraid or physically hurts you. Maybe like me, you find hope and comfort in books and fantasy. So many of us share this upbringing, and yet we've been taught to hide it. As Sam thinks in the book, *Never talk*.

It took me years to find a way into this story. To discover Sam and her sister Caitlin and to find a way to talk about their feelings of isolation and helplessness. And then, while I was designing a card game just for fun, I got an idea: the metaphor of abuse as a game with dangerous, ever-changing rules. It was a way to talk about Sam and Caitlin and their parents—and to show how abuse follows us even when we are physically out of harm's way—without losing the most critical element of the book.

Because on my first phone call with my editor, Tiff Liao, she asked me that question: What is the most important thing about this book, the heart that you don't want to lose in revisions? I told her it was the sense of hope. The assurance that there *is* a light at the end of the tunnel, a path out of the forest, a home where every person can experience unconditional love.

If you or someone you know is in a situation like Sam's, it can be difficult to ask for help. I've included resources at GameofFoxandSquirrels.com, as well as support for further conversations about the abuse portrayed in the novel.

If you're in a dark place, I hope this story resonates with you and gives you a bright, shining *Golden Acorn* to hold on to. And if you don't share Sam's experience with abuse, I hope her story gives you a new way to understand and empathize with those who do.

Thank you so much for reading.

ACKNOWLEDGMENTS

When I say "friends are my religion," I'm not being glib; I wouldn't be the person or the writer that I am if I didn't have these incredible people in my life. And I certainly wouldn't have written this book, which I have needed to write my entire life and which was the hardest, best, scariest, most fun, and most difficult story I have ever told.

Thank you to Stephanie Burgis, Tina Connolly, Christopher East, Ingrid Law, and Sarah Prineas. You folks are amazing and I want to bake you acorn-meat tarts.

For advice, critiques, emotional pep talks, and making me laugh when I most needed it, thank you to Marla Bowie, Rae Carson, Ted Chiang, Deborah Coates, Haddayr Copley-Woods, Deva Fagan, Sally Felt, Charlie Finlay, Christine Fletcher, Miriam Forster, Kelly Garrett, Marcia Glover, Claudia Hoffman, Rachael K. Jones, Samantha Ling, Karen Meisner, Lisa Moore, Ruth Musgrave, Anne Nesbet, Andrew Penn Romine, Carol Penn-Romine, Sara Ryan, Lisa Schroeder, Jen Udden, Greg van Eekhout, Cat Winters, Caroline M. Yoachim, and Trace Yulie.

My editor, Tiffany Liao, is so brilliant and funny and kind

that I'm perpetually in awe. She saw into the deepest core of what I was trying to say with this story and helped me find a better way to say it. It's an incredible gift to feel safe in someone's hands—especially with a story like this—and I did. I could not be more grateful for the time we spent collaborating on this huge piece of my heart.

I am deeply thankful to Mallory Grigg, Cynthia Lliguichuzhca, Olivia Oleck, Mark Podesta, Jordin Streeter, and the rest of the Henry Holt team for treating this book (and me) with such great care. And what a dream to see art by Jessica Roux alongside my words!

Thanks to Barry and Tricia.

Thanks to Holly and Alyssa at Root Literary.

Lastly, thanks to all the members of my found family, whether I mentioned them here or not. I'm so glad I don't have to do any of this alone.